FEATHER

M. G. LEONARD

WALKER
BOOKS

First published 2024 by Walker Books Ltd
87 Vauxhall Walk, London SE11 5HJ

2 4 6 8 10 9 7 5 3 1

Text © 2024 MG Leonard Ltd
Cover illustrations © 2024 Paddy Donnelly
Map illustrations © 2021 and 2024 Laurissa Jones

The right of M. G. Leonard to be identified as author of
this work has been asserted in accordance with
the Copyright, Designs and Patents Act 1988

This book has been typeset in Berkeley and Futura

Printed and bound by CPI Group (UK) Ltd, Croydon CR0 4YY

British Library Cataloguing in Publication Data:
a catalogue record for this book is available from the British Library

ISBN 978-1-5295-0611-2

www.walker.co.uk

MIX
Paper | Supporting
responsible forestry
FSC® C171272

For Kasper, always loved, never forgotten.

"Leave no black plume as a token of that lie
thy soul hath spoken!"
– Edgar Allan Poe, "The Raven"

"...all living things were not made for man."
– Alfred Russel Wallace,
The Annotated Malay Archipelago

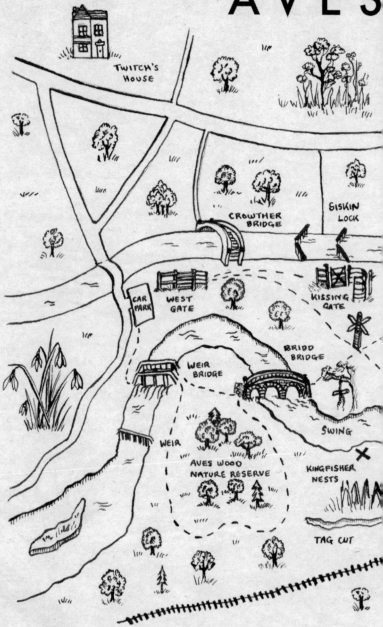

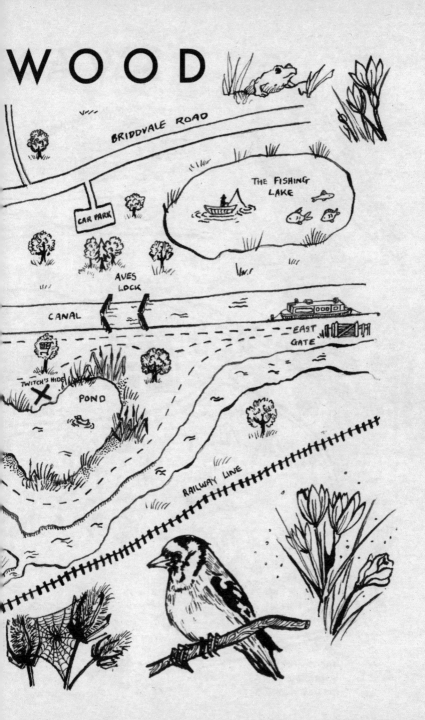

SWAN

TRAIN STATION

STATION CAFE

CAR PARK

POLICE STATION

CHURCH

PLAYGROUND

CAR PARK

BUS STOP

PICNIC TABLES

THE SWAN NATURAL HISTORY MUSEUM

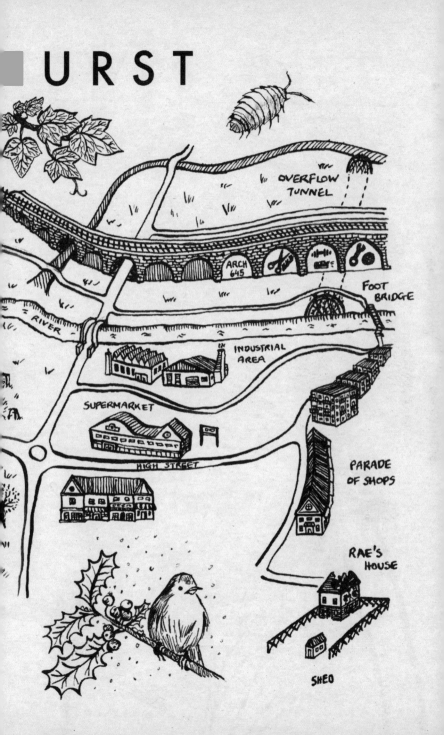

1

BIRDS OF PARADISE

Museums are places the living go to think about things that are dead, Ava thought as she wiped condensation from the window with her fist. The school coach was parking outside an old manor house; she was looking at a pair of stone columns, supporting a porch, framing a giant wooden door. There was a sign hammered into the lawn that read: *THE SWAN NATURAL HISTORY MUSEUM*. The place looked creepy.

The school trip was supposed to be a treat before the half-term holiday, but Ava couldn't wait for it to be over.

"Gather on the grass outside," Ms Frank called as the coach door opened.

Ava's classmates began pushing and shoving their way down the aisle. She waited until the crush had passed before getting off herself. The fresh air was a cold shock. The veil of drowsiness, created by the body heat of forty-five teenagers and the motion of a travelling coach, was whipped away by the freezing temperature. The pavement glittered with frost particles. The grass was dressed with ice. A shiver climbed Ava's spine. She folded her black-and-purple blazer across her chest, hugging it round her as she glanced up. The sky was a pale stone white and clear of clouds. A pair of jackdaws with pewter-grey heads and bandit-like eye markings watched them from the skeletal crown of a dormant silver birch.

"Listen, please." Ms Frank's chestnut curls bounced as she stepped down from the coach. "Get into your groups. Mr Barnes will give each of you a clipboard with the scavenger hunt on it as you go into the museum. First group back with the right answers gets a prize." She tipped her head. "Everyone got that?"

A series of grunts, affirmative murmurs, and the shuffling of feet was her reply.

"We'll meet in the lobby at twelve-thirty for lunch." She glanced at the museum entrance to make sure Mr Barnes was in position with his box of clipboards. "Off you go."

Ava moved away with the rest of her class. Feeling her phone vibrate in her pocket, she slid it out, speedily scanning the message from her best friend, Tara, and smiled to herself as she put the phone away. She and Tara, along with Jack, Terry, Ozuru, Twitch and her nine-year-old sister Tippi, were part of a group of birdwatching detectives called the Twitchers. Tara's message had said that they would all be at the station tomorrow morning to meet her when her train arrived in Briddvale, and that Jack was desperately trying to find a crime for them to solve during the February half-term holiday.

The thought of seeing her friends tomorrow and staying a whole week at Tara's triggered a warm glow inside Ava that eased the chill of the winter morning.

She took a clipboard as she passed Mr Barnes and joined Nadine, Jenny and Sarah, who were waiting for her in the tiled lobby of the museum.

"Look at these questions," Nadine was complaining. "Find a case of birds that feed on insects, and complete the food chain diagram. How are we supposed to know which birds eat bugs?"

"So dull." Jenny sighed as she flicked through the pages.

"Passerines," Ava said, her mind still on the Twitchers.

"What?" Nadine and Jenny looked at her. The girls were best friends and practically the same person. They both had high ponytails, twinkly stud earrings, badges on the lapels of their blazers, and bags decorated with dangling keychains of fluffy goggle-eyed creatures.

"Perching birds, like finches, sparrows and starlings," Ava explained, not sure which of them to look at. "I mean, lots of birds eat bugs – most of them, actually – but we're probably looking for a case of small songbirds."

There was an awkward silence. Sarah, who was a nervous girl and eager to please, blurted out, "Who even cares about" – she glanced at the scavenger hunt – "Ecosystems and Food Webs! I mean … so boring!" She snorted as she chuckled.

"Everyone should," Ava replied flatly, feeling annoyed with herself that she'd mentioned passerines. She usually avoided the complicated politics of school relationships by keeping her mouth shut. "If food chains break down, the planet's ecosystem collapses, and we'll all die."

"Yeah, Sarah," Nadine said.

"Yeah, Sarah," Jenny echoed.

"Erm, I think we need to go this way." Ava pointed, trying not to notice the crestfallen expression on Sarah's face.

Nadine and Jenny led the way, ponytails swinging. Ava tried to walk beside Sarah, who scowled and picked up her pace to catch up with the other girls. Not for the first time, Ava wondered why she didn't seem to be able to get on with the kids at her school. She had joined Mountview Secondary in September, after they'd moved house. Her mum had wanted a fresh start for them all after she'd been released from prison. Yet, somehow, rumours about Ava's family had crept through the school. She'd heard the whispering; some of it wasn't very quiet.

Whereas she'd met the Twitchers in the previous summer; they knew what had happened to her mum and it had never been a problem. Her friends in Briddvale were different and she missed them intensely. She imagined her train pulling up at the station tomorrow morning and seeing their delighted faces as she got off. She couldn't wait to take the path into Aves Wood and follow the rabbit track below the shopping trolley tree to their secret hide.

Ava blinked. Nadine, Jenny and Sarah were no longer in front of her. They'd vanished. Two open doors led off the cavernous hall; above one was a sign saying: *CREATURES THAT MADE HISTORY.* There was a staircase in front of her with a lift beside it. Gazing up, Ava could see the low balcony wall of each level and it occurred to her that it might be more fun to complete the scavenger hunt on her own. She pressed the button to call the lift, which was on level three. She stepped inside. She'd start at the top of the building and work her way down.

The silver doors opened and Ava came out on level five. She saw glass cases containing stuffed birds, but the gallery was empty of people. A sign informed her that this was the Birds of the World exhibit. Her footsteps echoed off the polished wooden floor as she approached a cabinet the size of a shop window. The exhibition was divided into sections, a different type of bird in each. The glass eyes and straw innards of the dead birds made them look like puppets. Ava felt goosebumps rising on her body as she passed along the display. She preferred birds to be alive.

Drawn towards an arrangement of brightly coloured passerines on perches, she read the white plaque in the case: *PARADISAEIDAE – BIRDS OF PARADISE, COLLECTED BY ALFRED RUSSEL WALLACE, 1857.* She blinked, astonished to realize that these were the very birds Wallace had described in his book about the Malay Archipelago. Twitch had told her about the enigmatic birds that lived, hidden and protected, in the rainforests of New Guinea. It was his dream to one day make the expedition to see their dazzling displays and curious courtship dances. His dog-eared copy of Alfred Russel Wallace's book lived in the hide. Ava had dipped into it many times.

Reaching into her pocket, Ava got her fingers around her phone, thinking she'd take a photo to show Twitch, when a long, high whistle, followed by a piercing alarm, sliced through the dusty silence. Startled, she dropped her clipboard, letting out a cry of surprise.

Spinning around, Ava searched for a reason for the noise. Her heart was racing. Fear made her skin prickle. She was alone in the gallery.

Running to one of the arched windows, Ava looked out. She thought it must be a fire alarm but she couldn't see smoke.

She sniffed the air. Nothing.

People below were hurrying out of the museum looking concerned. Ava spotted Ms Frank waving at the children from her school. Mr Barnes was counting heads and taking a register. She should join them.

Hurrying back to Wallace's birds, Ava grabbed her clipboard, shoving it into her rucksack, yanked her phone from her pocket and snapped a photo, feeling a pang at the thought of Alfred Russel Wallace's birds being burned.

"They're already dead, Ava," she muttered. "Get moving before you are too."

The alarm seemed to be ringing inside her head. With a lurch she remembered she was at the top of the building – the worst place to be if there was a fire. She knew not to use the lift. That could be a death trap. She needed to find the stairs.

Hearing a door slam and running footsteps, Ava pivoted. At the far end of the gallery was a corridor; beside it was a sign saying *NO PUBLIC ACCESS*. To the right she spotted a staircase with a green fire exit sign. She sprinted to it and down to level four.

Through a window, Ava glimpsed three police cars pulling up, blue lights flashing, officers leaping from their vehicles. She paused. They'd got here fast! Where were the fire engines? She heard no more approaching sirens. A security guard jogged out of the building, waving the police inside, and the alarm suddenly fell silent.

Ava's skin prickled.

The people milling about below looked disgruntled. They didn't look afraid or alarmed. Surely if there was a fire, the police would be outside setting up a cordon, not going inside.

Still no fire engines.

Was it a false alarm? Had Freddy Rigby set the fire alarm off on purpose, like he did in school? But then, wouldn't the police be questioning the people outside?

Maybe it hadn't been a fire alarm at all.

Ava was suddenly alert. Her ears were pricked up. Her eyes were wide.

What if it was a burglar alarm?

She knew some burglar alarms were connected to police stations. It made sense that the museum's would be.

What if there was a crime taking place in the building right now?

2
THE DARWIN DECOY

I could take a quick scout around, Ava thought, pulling a scrunchie from her blazer pocket and tying her mane of black curls into a top knot. It would do no harm to investigate. It might help the police. Pushing open the door to level four, she scanned the gallery for any sign of thieves, all the while sniffing the air for fire. If she detected a whiff of smoke, she'd run.

Darting from case to cabinet, Ava peered into every corner but saw nothing. Below her, she could hear the distant clatter of running feet and barked orders.

Where had the alarm been triggered? It must be in a different part of the museum? This was the geology floor. The case nearest to her contained fossils. It didn't appear to be alarmed but it was locked. Perhaps the museum only put alarms on cases containing valuable things. Ava felt a thrill at the idea that something priceless might have been stolen from the museum whilst she was in it. Jack would be so impressed when she told him.

Satisfied that there were no clues or robbers to be found on level four, Ava returned to the staircase and quickly descended to level three. As she crept into the exhibition hall, she heard a quiet sound, like fabric brushing against fabric, followed by the rustle of plastic. She stiffened, trying to tune in to the sound and identify where it was coming from.

Dropping into a squat, she crept and crawled through the hall, hiding and peeping around cabinets containing polar bears and penguins, closing in on the noise. The police were getting louder. She leaned her back against a display case containing a disgruntled walrus and closed her eyes, straining to hear, but the commotion of the police officers and security guards searching the floor below eclipsed all other sounds.

Concerned she would lose the source of the noise, Ava dashed, bent double, to the end of the room. She saw a corridor cordoned off by a rope and a sign saying *AUTHORIZED ACCESS ONLY*. Down the wood-panelled wall of the corridor was a door. A brass plaque above it said: *THE WALLACE ROOM*. The door was ajar.

The people inside probably heard the alarm and ran, Ava reasoned. Or, there could be someone in there committing a crime right now!

She tiptoed to the rope, ducked under, and sidled up to the door. She held her breath as she peered through the gap.

The room was empty.

Exhaling a disappointed puff of relief, Ava went inside. She found herself standing in a wood-panelled room lined with cupboards. There weren't any windows or pictures on the walls. It was a fancy storage cupboard. She turned to leave, feeling deflated, but was stopped by an odd sight.

On the floor, in front of the cupboard behind the door, was a large black feather.

"What are you doing in here?" Ava whispered, picking up the feather and twirling it. She ran her finger along the inky veins. It didn't look like an old feather. It shimmered with newness. The only birds in the museum were dead, stuffed and in cases, their feathers showing signs of dryness and fading. This looked like it had come from some sort of crow.

Pulling out her clipboard, Ava lifted the scavenger hunt sheet and trapped the feather beneath it.

"It could be just a feather," she told herself, sliding

the clipboard into her bag. "Or, it could be a clue!" Her heart bounced at this thought.

Footsteps in the exhibit hall made Ava pivot, looking for a place to hide.

"None of Darwin's finches are missing," a man said. "Your curator has checked. They are going through the rest of the exhibition now."

"Thank goodness," replied a woman with a gravelly voice.

"It looks like someone tried to break into the display case. A metal rod was found inserted into the lock. When they couldn't pick it, they tried to smash the glass with a rock. That's what set off the alarm."

"So they were after the finches?"

"Looks likely," he went on. "There's a broken window on the ground floor. The rubber seal around the glazing has been levered out. The glass fell and smashed on the path. But it's a small window – too small for an adult to have climbed through. It might not be related."

"Which window is it?"

"In the public toilets, at the back of the building."

"The ones that look out onto the wooded picnic spot?"

In the silence, Ava guessed the man was nodding.

"Officers are checking the area."

There were more footsteps.

"Is anything missing?" the woman with the gravelly voice asked.

"The curators are double-checking the rooms around the Creatures That Made History exhibit," a young woman's voice replied, "but it doesn't look like it."

"Thank you for coming so swiftly, Chief Superintendent," the woman with the gravelly voice said. "Friday is when we have visiting school groups and it is often full of … shall we say … mishaps, but never before an attempted robbery."

"Not a problem," the man said. "Although we haven't ruled out this being a mishap. The attempt to get into the finches' case wasn't professional. It looks like the work of an amateur."

"Will I be able to let the visitors back into the museum today?" the young woman asked.

"Possibly, but only once we've completed a thorough search of the museum," replied the Chief Superintendent. "That will take some time."

Ava frowned as they walked away. If the thief had failed to break into the case of Darwin's finches, why would they smash the toilet window to escape? Surely they would simply walk out of the museum with the other members of the public? And if the thief had fled

24

the moment the alarm was triggered, then who or what had she heard in here?

Nobody had searched the room she was in yet. She considered the tall cabinets that lined the walls. What was in them anyway?

Covering her hand with her school jumper, so as not to leave fingerprints, Ava tugged at the handle of the closest cupboard door, expecting it to be locked. It opened. Inside was a stack of white drawers. Pulling at one, she saw it was empty except for two dead brown birds at the back. Peering at the white labels attached to their legs, she saw they were female birds of paradise. She guessed this room must house the rest of Alfred Russel Wallace's collection of birds, the ones not on display upstairs in the Birds of the World exhibit.

She touched her finger to the tail feathers of one of the brown birds. This small creature connected her to one of the greatest naturalists in all of history. She pulled another drawer open, hungry to see more. It was empty. The missing birds must be the ones she'd seen upstairs, although the Birds of the World display case had only featured one bird of each species. The label on this drawer suggested it should contain multiple birds of a single species. She opened another drawer. It too was empty. Ava felt a lurch of alarm as she pulled open three more drawers. They were all empty.

Thinking of the black feather in her rucksack, Ava checked the labels on the drawers, but none of them said *Corvidae*. She remembered the strange sound that had brought her to this room. Could it have been the sound of bird skins being hurriedly shoved into a carrier bag?

Had the alarm been a decoy? Was this the true crime scene? Had the thief been after the Alfred Russel Wallace bird skins all along?

She needed to tell the police!

Ava dashed into the gallery, sprinting to the staircase, rushing down the steps two at a time, all the while thinking about the moment the strange rustling noise had stopped.

Where had she been?

With a shiver of fear, Ava realized the thief must have passed by her on the other side of the cabinet with the walrus in it!

As she stumbled into the lobby, out of breath, Ava saw a uniformed man with grey hair and an air of authority was standing in the museum entrance, shaking hands with a woman in a toffee-coloured skirt and jacket as if he was leaving. "Stop!" she called out. "Wait!"

"Are you looking for your school group?" An eager-faced young officer stepped in front of Ava. "They're out the front by the coaches."

"No, you don't understand. There's been a robbery!"

"We've got it all in hand." The officer motioned for her to move towards the door. "No need to worry."

Ava walked towards the door, but when the officer turned his back, she changed direction, running to the woman. "Please. You must listen to me. Wallace's birds of paradise are gone. They've been stolen!"

"I beg your pardon?" The woman in the toffee-coloured suit blinked. Ava recognized her gravelly tone as the woman she'd heard speaking to the Chief Superintendent upstairs.

"The drawers in the Wallace Room… They're empty!"

"Who are you?" The woman frowned. "What were you doing in the Wallace Room?" Her tone was sharp. "It's out of bounds to the public. It's locked."

"It's not locked." Ava could feel herself getting hot.

"No collector would steal the Wallace birds when Darwin's finches are in the building," the woman said, almost to reassure herself. She glanced at the Chief Superintendent. "Darwin's birds are invaluable." She gave a shake of her head and frowned at Ava. "The drawer you looked in must've been the one we took specimens from for the Birds of the World display."

"No, I've seen that. Way more birds are missing. More than one drawer is empty. Lots of them are."

"What?" The woman was looking alarmed now.

"I found a clue in the Wallace Room, on the floor," Ava told the Chief Superintendent, who raised a whiskery eyebrow. "It's a large black feather. It looks like it could be from a crow."

"Really?" The Chief Superintendent suppressed a smile. "Well, you've been very helpful," he replied with a wink. "Now, you should return to your classmates. They'll be wondering where you are."

"Don't you want the feather?"

"Why don't you keep it as a souvenir?" The old Chief Superintendent smiled at her, and Ava realized he wasn't taking her seriously.

"Fine," she snapped, walking towards the exit. "But I'm not the one who fell for the Darwin decoy. When you go up to the Wallace Room, you'll see that you all did!"

3

THE RAVEN

Standing on the doorstep of the museum, Ava glanced back. The woman, Chief Superintendent and the young officer were hurrying up the stairs. Quick as a flash, Ava darted back inside. She couldn't investigate the Darwin exhibit – it would be crawling with curators – but she might be able to investigate the broken window before the police realized there had been a theft and the whole museum became a crime scene.

Moving slowly with her back against the lift, Ava sidled into the stairwell that led down to the lower ground floor. A police officer was talking to a museum security guard in front of the corridor to the public toilets. Keeping low, she crept to the opposite wall and inched round the corner, behind them.

"To be honest, we're not the kind of place that gets broken into," the security guard was saying. "And no one in their right mind would break a window to climb in when they can walk through the front door? Entry is free, you know. My money's on one of those schoolkids smashing it. That happens."

"The Super thinks it's a false alarm," the police officer agreed. "Nothing's been nicked."

As soon as she was out of view, Ava sprinted to the toilets, not daring to look back. The criminals had been clever to use the Darwin alarm as a distraction. Who knows how long it would've taken someone to notice the drawers in the Wallace Room were empty if she hadn't gone in there? An hour? Maybe longer. Ava was one step ahead of the police and she wanted to keep it that way. A corridor took her into a room with a row of cubicles opposite a line of sinks. Above one of the sinks was the missing window.

Pulling out her phone, Ava took a photo of the empty casement. Looking around, she could see no sign of what had broken it: no stone or tool or weapon. Poking her head through the hole, she saw smashed glass on the concrete path outside. She snapped a picture. Under the glass was a black strip and Ava remembered the Chief Superintendent saying the rubber seal had been levered out. The way the glass had landed made Ava think it had been pushed from inside, but if the rubber seal had been pulled out, maybe the thief had prized out the glass from outside. But then why let it smash on the ground? That would make a noise and draw attention. And the security guard was right: why come in via the window when entrance to the museum was free?

Was the window a red herring? Or was it an escape route?

The casement wasn't big, but Ava reckoned she could get out of it. Pulling her sleeves over her hands, she clambered onto the sink and slid through, dropping to the path. Her feet crunched on the broken glass. She looked at the window from the outside. She didn't think anyone much bigger than her could have got through it. She took another photo.

"If I were a thief and I came this way, where would I go next?" Ava looked across the lawn, immediately drawing back against the brick wall as two police officers came running across the grass, their ears pressed to the radios on their protective vests.

The missing birds must have been discovered.

Peering across the lawn, beyond a group of picnic tables, Ava saw a winding path edged with snowdrops. It led into a wood that looked like a pen and ink drawing: black trunks, bare branches, white sky. Might the thieves be hiding in there?

Checking the coast was clear, Ava sprinted across the lawn.

"Ava Kingfisher!" Ms Frank's voice stopped her in her tracks. "I've been looking everywhere for you."

Ava winced at the tone of her teacher's voice. It was then that she became aware of a pair of beady black eyes staring at her from the low branch of a chestnut tree on the fringe of the wood.

A raven!

Ava locked eyes with the ebony bird and thought of the feather in her bag.

"Come here this instant," Ms Frank insisted.

The brooding raven had eyes like a demon, wicked and wise. With a shiver, Ava did as she was told. She glanced back. The ominous bird was watching her.

"Sorry, Ms Frank," Ava mumbled as she drew near the harassed teacher.

"What on earth are you doing back here?" Ms Frank was cross. "I've been through the register twice. I thought we'd lost you! I was about to ask the police to look for you."

"I'm sorry, Ms Frank. I didn't mean to worry you," Ava said, apologetically. "I was birdwatching."

"We'll discuss this when we get back to school." Ms Frank motioned Ava to walk in front of her.

"Yes, Ms Frank."

As they walked around the building, Ava couldn't shake the image of the watching raven. Did the feather in her rucksack belong to that bird? Surely that was unlikely. What would a wild raven be doing inside a museum? It could hardly have been the thief.

When they reached the coach, half her class were on board. With nothing else to do, they were eating their packed lunches.

"I see you found her," Mr Barnes said with a shake of his head. "Whilst you were away, a police officer informed me that they won't be letting anyone back in the museum today. We must cancel the trip."

Ava kept her face blank and her eyes on the ground.

"What a disaster," Ms Frank sighed. "Well, let's round everyone up and get them back on the coach. You first, Ava."

Ava nodded, suppressing a smile as she pictured the excitement of the Twitchers tomorrow when she told them that she had a case for them to solve. She couldn't wait to reveal that she had been the one to discover the crime scene.

An idea flashed into her head. What if she was to go to Briddvale today instead of tomorrow? Swanhurst was only about a forty-minute drive from Briddvale. It was a big town – it must have a railway station. She had the money she'd brought for the museum gift shop. She could catch a train!

She felt a crackle of excitement.

"There are thirty-one children on the coach," Mr Barnes told Ms Frank. "Ava makes thirty-two. The rest of them are over there." He pointed across the car park to a bench beneath a giant oak tree where Nadine and Jenny were holding court.

"I'll get on the coach shall I, Ms Frank?" Ava said.

"Hmm? Yes. Climb aboard, Ava." Ms Frank nodded, and Ava made sure her teacher saw her climb the stairs.

Hovering in the aisle by the driver's seat, Ava watched Ms Frank and Mr Barnes set out to round up the group of students around the bench.

She let out a mumbled exclamation as if she'd forgotten something and hurried back down the coach steps. Rushing to the front of the vehicle, she squatted down behind one of its enormous wheels. She looked about for a hiding place but was surrounded by flat lawn and thin trees. Panic fluttered in her chest as she heard her classmates approach the coach and board. She needed to move!

Beyond the car park, across the road, was a playground. On the pavement in front of it was a bus stop. Sitting on the bench inside was a kid about her own age, a skinny figure in black, with straight hair centrally parted, hanging like half-closed curtains in front of her face.

Launching into a sprint, Ava charged across the car park and over the road to the bus stop.

"Hi. My name's Ava," she said, wrenching off her rucksack and wriggling behind the bench. "I'm going to hide down here. Please don't give me away."

"You in trouble?" the girl asked in a muted voice.

"No, no. Nothing like that. I just don't want to go back to school."

"OK," the girl replied, as if this made perfect sense.

"Will you tell me when that coach has driven away?"

"Sure."

Squatting soon became uncomfortable. Ava shifted, trying to find a better position. When the coach engine roared into life, her heart gave a tiny hiccup of fear. Unable to see, Ava stared at the girl, hoping her expression might give some clue as to what was happening. But the girl's chin was thrust forward and her stare blank. Ava saw the purple shadow of a faded bruise around her right eye and wondered how she'd got it.

"Stay down," the girl muttered. "The coach is coming out of the car park."

Ava felt her phone vibrate in her pocket but didn't dare pull it out. She heard the growl of the approaching vehicle and held her breath as it passed.

"Don't get up yet," warned the girl. "They'll see you in the rear-view mirror."

Ava listened as her classmates disappeared down the road, on their way back to school.

"All clear."

"Thanks!" Ava popped up from behind the bench, unable to keep the grin from her face. She yanked her phone from her pocket. The message was from Tara, asking what time her train was getting into Briddvale the next day.

"Do you know if there is a station near here?"

"Yeah." The girl pointed in the direction the coach had travelled. "It's that way."

"Do you know how long it takes to walk there?"

"About half an hour."

"Brilliant. Er…" Ava found she wasn't sure what to say to the girl. She didn't know her name. "Thanks for helping."

"No problem." The girl turned away from Ava, looking up the road as if expecting her bus to arrive at any moment.

"Bye then," Ava said, typing a message into her phone as she walked away:

Change of plan! I'm coming TODAY!!! Got a case for the Twitchers! And it is a BIG ONE! A x

A case? How? Aren't you at school? T x

Will explain. Am on my way. Will let you know when I'm on a train. A x

BRILLIANT! I'll tell the others. School breaks up at lunch today. We can meet you at the station. T x

Ava started to jog. As she ran, more police cars passed her on their way to the museum. She couldn't help feeling proud to have been the one who'd discovered the theft. She knew Jack would be impressed.

It occurred to Ava that her mum might be cross that she'd slipped away from the school coach. She would call and explain once she was on the train to Briddvale. After all, she was thirteen and it wasn't her fault the school trip was cancelled.

Realizing that her holiday had started, Ava felt a rush of freedom. Her little sister, Tippi, was away at a school residential. She didn't get back until Sunday, which meant Ava had two Tippi-free days in Briddvale. She loved her sister but had to take care of her when they stayed with Tara. Right now, she had no responsibilities and an incredible mystery to solve: a museum heist!

4

THE FEATHER HEIST

As her train approached Briddvale Station, Ava's spirits lifted. Her mum had been horribly cross with her. She wasn't happy about calling the school to explain why Ava wasn't on the coach. She'd told Ava that another stunt like this would mean no more unsupervised trips to see her friends and Ava had apologized repeatedly. Eventually her mum had calmed down, making her promise to be good for Tara's parents.

Springing up from her seat, Ava looked for her friends through the window in the train door. The sky was overcast and threatening rain. The doors opened. Stepping down to the platform, she saw Tara and Jack running towards her.

"Ava!" Tara cried, her long black hair flying out behind her, with a wide smile on her face. "We came straight from school."

"What's the crime?" Jack asked, fixing his green eyes on her. "You said there was a crime to solve – what is it? I'm dying to know."

"Jack!" Tara smacked his arm lightly. "Ava's just got here." Linking her arm through Ava's, Tara walked towards the exit. "Everyone's meeting at Twitch's house to hear your news."

"I saw your message to Tara," Jack said, hurrying to Ava's side. "The case – is it juicy?"

"Can't you wait?" Tara sounded exasperated.

"I need to know." He clasped his hands together and his voice took on a pleading tone. "Don't torture me, Ava. I can't take it."

"I suppose I could tell you…" Ava teased. She felt a spot of rain on her head and looked up, holding out her hand. "Hey, is it raining?"

Tara pulled an umbrella from the side pocket of her school bag.

"Who cares about rain?" Jack groaned.

"Actually," Tara said, opening the umbrella as icy needles bombarded them, "I think it's sleet."

"Kill me. Kill me now!" Jack threw out his arms dramatically, letting sleet pelt him. "I can't take this torture!"

"All right!" Ava laughed, grabbing him and

yanking him under the umbrella. "I'll tell you… It's a museum heist."

"A museum heist?" A look of awe dawned on Jack's face. "Really? Which museum? When?"

"Today. The Swan Museum in Swanhurst." Ava paused. "I was there when it happened. I discovered the scene of the crime."

"What?" Jack looked like he was struggling not to swallow his own tongue. "You have to tell me everything. Immediately!"

"Jack." Tara's voice had a warning tone. "Everyone is waiting to hear Ava's news. It's not fair if you hear it first."

"But…" Ava tried not to smile as Jack struggled to find a good argument. "What if I die before then?"

Ava laughed and hugged Tara's arm to her. "I've missed you guys." It felt great to be back with her friends.

"I've missed you too." Tara beamed at her. "When you and Tippi aren't here, I'm the only girl and *that*" – she eyeballed Jack – "can be infuriating."

"Fine, I mean, you don't have to tell me everything" – Jack bumped into Ava as the three of them tried to stay under the umbrella – "but surely there's something…" He looked hopefully at her.

"All right." Ava chuckled. "I will tell you that I found a clue."

"A clue? What was it? Does it point at a suspect? Do you have any suspects? It would really help to know exactly what the crime was. You said it was a heist, so I'm guessing a theft, but what was stolen? Were the police there? Are they investigating? Of course they are. I wonder if it's going to be on the news."

Ava lifted her chin to show that she wouldn't be saying another word until they were at Twitch's house.

"Oh, come on!" Jack stopped walking, but only for two seconds because the sleet drummed on his skull, plastering his spiky hair over his forehead.

Despite the umbrella, all three of them were soaked and shivering by the time they reached Twitch's front door.

Ozuru had spotted them coming up the road and was standing in the open doorway grinning. They hurried inside. Twitch handed Jack a towel as they took their shoes and coats off.

"Do you want some hot blackcurrant squash?" Ozuru asked. "We've already boiled the kettle."

"Yes, please." Ava nodded. Her legs felt like icicles.

"On it!" Twitch dashed off, returning with a tray of five steaming cups. He put it down on the coffee table in the living room.

Ava liked the homeliness of Twitch's faded furniture and the quaint paintings of birds that hung on the walls. It was a comfy room that wouldn't tell on you if you accidentally spilled or scratched something. Seeing the gas fire was on, she went and stood in front of it to warm up the backs of her legs. Her socks were wet through and she couldn't feel her toes. "Where's Terry?" she asked, looking around.

"At Pam's," Jack replied as he dried his wet hair with the towel.

"Pamela Hardacre's?" Ava had not expected him to say that.

"Ozuru thinks they might be secretly boyfriend and girlfriend," Tara said.

"What?" Ava's jaw dropped. "But Terry HATES Pam!"

"And yet," Twitch said, "right now he's at her house helping her set up her new computer."

"Terry doesn't know anything about computers." Ozuru crossed his arms. He and Terry were best friends and Ava could see that he wasn't happy about this new relationship.

"Does he know I'm here?" Ava asked. "With a case that needs solving?"

"We told him," Jack said. "He said he would come … as soon as he'd finished helping Pam!"

"Wow." Ava tried not to feel offended. "I don't believe it."

"Yesterday, after school," Ozuru told her, "he said he needed to run an errand for his mum, but he lied. I followed him all the way to Pam's house."

"He lied to you?" Ava frowned. It didn't sound like Terry.

"Anyway, enough of Terry's love life." Jack dropped the towel to the floor and rubbed his hands together. "Let's hear about the case!"

"In a sec," Ava said, picking up her cup of hot blackcurrant and taking a slurp.

Jack wailed, falling back into an armchair, and everyone laughed.

"OK." Ava sat down on the rug, wrapping her hands around her mug. "This is what happened."

She began with her decision to do the scavenger hunt on her own, and going up to the fifth level of the museum. "They have a display up there with birds of paradise." She looked at Twitch. "Some of them are the actual birds that Alfred Russel Wallace collected."

"I've seen it." Twitch nodded. "They're incredible."

"I thought you hated displays of dead birds," Ozuru said.

"Museums are different," Twitch said. "They have

43

a collection that everyone can go and look at to learn about birds. If people don't learn about birds, they won't care to protect them. Some of the birds in the Swan collection are already extinct. They're a warning." He paused, thinking for a moment. "Back when Wallace collected his birds, there was no other way to record a species. There were no cameras. And they weren't endangered. They were new wonders. Wallace's generation discovered birds. Our generation must save them." He sighed. "That's why I get angry when people destroy precious habitats or shoot birds for sport and keep creepy cases of them in their house."

Ava thought about the cases of stuffed birds in Mord Hall and nodded. "What do you know about Darwin's finches?" she asked Twitch.

"Charles Darwin collected them when he was on the HMS *Beagle*, exploring the Galapagos Islands," Twitch replied. "The finches all have different beak shapes because of what they eat. They're the evidence that supports Darwin's theory of natural selection, and the theory of evolution. They're probably the most important birds in human history."

"They are in the Swan Museum," Ava said.

"Yes." Twitch nodded.

"Forget boring old Darwin and tell us about the

crime!" Jack insisted. "You were up looking at birds when..." He waved his hand at her encouragingly.

"An alarm went off," Ava told him. "I thought it was a fire alarm. I searched for the stairs and the fire exit, but then I saw police cars arrive and officers running into the building."

She described how she'd discovered the theft in the Wallace Room, feeling a surge of pleasure as the others leaned forward, drinking in every word. Ozuru was scribbling down notes. Twitch had a faraway look in his eyes. Tara was shaking her head. And Jack looked like he might explode.

"I don't understand," Tara said. "Why would anyone want to steal dead birds?"

"These aren't just any birds," Ava said. "These are birds of paradise. Some of them were collected by Alfred Russel Wallace himself! He's one of the greatest naturalists in history."

"But still..." Tara looked doubtful. "Why? I mean, that curator lady said herself, Darwin's finches are more valuable. Why not steal those?"

"Maybe the finches were impossible to get at," Ozuru said, "in the alarmed case."

"Perhaps someone wanted pretty feathers," Jack suggested. "They're brightly coloured birds. Maybe the robbery was done by a fashion designer with a feather fixation."

"Like *101 Dalmatians* but instead of puppy coats, they want colourful feathers?" Ava shrugged. "It's possible."

"This is a feather heist," Jack declared. "And the Twitchers were the first at the scene. We discovered this crime and we're going to solve it."

"Yes." Ava pulled her rucksack towards her, sliding out her clipboard and producing the large black feather. "And this is our first clue!"

5
THE DANCING BABOON

Ozuru's phone lit up and he answered it. "Hi, Terry… What?" He rolled his eyes and sighed. "Fine. I'll tell them. Bye."

"Terry's going to be a while," he said. "Apparently, setting up Pam's computer is taking ages."

"Probably all the smooching they're doing is getting in the way." Jack made a kissing noise.

"Ew, Jack!" Tara pulled a face. "Gross!"

"Why don't we go to Pam's?" Ava suggested.

"What for?" Ozuru asked.

"To find out what Terry's up to," Ava explained. "We can pretend that we need to use her computer because we don't want our parents to know we're working on a case."

"Actually, I'd rather my parents didn't know," Tara admitted.

"That's a genius idea." Twitch was grinning.

"We can't start this case without Terry," Ava said. "And we need to get online, to find out what kind of person wants bird skins badly enough to steal them from a museum."

"And if we go to Pam's we can do both," Tara said.

"But Pam will want in on the crime solving," Jack pointed out.

"She won't," Tara replied. "She only ever wants to report crimes, not solve them."

"I want to find out why Terry's been lying to me." Ozuru got to his feet.

"The first forty-eight hours after a crime are critical." Jack jumped up. "If you don't have a lead, a suspect, or an arrest within forty-eight hours, the trail goes cold. Your chances of solving a case are cut in half."

"It's decided then." Ava drained her cup. "Let's go to Pam's."

It was getting dark by the time they rang Pam's bell.

"Hi, Mrs Hardacre," Jack said, as Pam's mum opened the door. "We've come to help Pam set up her computer."

"Hello, Jack." She gave him a bemused smile. "That's very kind. Although, I thought Pammy had set up her computer weeks ago."

"Oh! Er, she did," Jack improvised. "She's having teething troubles."

"It's nice of you to help." Mrs Hardacre stood back, ushering them inside. "Pammy's studio is in the spare bedroom. Up the stairs to the right, at the end of the landing."

"Her studio?" Ava whispered to Tara.

"She's taking being a YouTuber very seriously," Tara replied as they entered the immaculate white house with champagne-coloured furnishings.

Jack led the way up the stairs, marching to the end of the landing, and pushing the door open without knocking. He froze, looking shocked. Curious, Ava peered past him into the room.

Terry was standing in front of a green backdrop, lit by a ring light, dressed as a cartoon bank robber with a black mask over his eyes and a giant sack swung over his back.

Pam was looking into a video camera and shouting, "Come on! Be menacing! You look like one of Santa's elves bringing presents! You're meant to be a criminal!"

"I'm trying." Terry turned and dropped the swag bag when he saw the Twitchers. "It's not what it looks like!" He held his hands up.

"Oh, it's you lot." Pam blew at a strand of blonde

49

hair that had fallen over her face. "What do you want? We're busy."

"I thought Terry was helping you set up your computer." Ozuru eyeballed Terry and he blushed.

"Oh please!" Pam's voice was dripping with disdain. "I know how to plug in a computer. I've had my editing station set up for ages."

"What *are* you doing?" Twitch asked, looking mystified.

"Acting!" Terry said, snatching off his burglar's eye mask.

"I needed some funny cutaways to spice up my news videos," Pam explained. "Terry volunteered."

"As if!" Terry folded his arms. "You filmed me on your phone doing … doing … something, and … and you said you were going to put it on YouTube if I didn't help you."

"And then you immediately volunteered!" Pam countered.

Tara suppressed a giggle.

"We're here on serious Twitchers business," Jack said importantly. "We need Terry. We've got a case to solve."

"A case?" Pam straightened up, a keen look in her eye.

"A big one," Ava told her. "A museum heist."

"What was stolen?" Pam's eyes sparkled. "Jewellery? Priceless art? Roman coins?"

"Really old bird skins," Twitch told her.

"Urgh!" Pam looked disappointed. "I should've known it wasn't a real crime. No one would steal a dead bird's skin."

"A bird skin holds all the feathers," Tara explained patiently. "It's the feathers that people want, not the skin."

"These are birds of paradise skins that Alfred Russel Wallace collected in the Malay Archipelago," Twitch told her.

"Russell Wally who?" Pam waved her hand as if swatting a fly. "Sounds boring. Can't you find a proper crime, like a murder or something? I need *good* stories for the channel." She pointed at Terry. "Why do you think I'm making him dance around like a baboon?"

"A baboon?" Terry glared at Pam. "That's rich coming from a … a … spider like you."

Pam turned away, acting as if she hadn't heard him. Terry silently mimed strangling her.

"I don't think you have to worry about them being boyfriend and girlfriend," Ava said to Ozuru with a chuckle.

Terry heard her and his mouth dropped open. He glared at Ozuru. "Girlfriend and boyfriend?"

"You lied to me," Ozuru retorted crossly. "How was I supposed to know what you were doing?"

"What did you think I was doing?" Terry asked.

"Kissing." Jack grinned.

"Ew, don't be disgusting!" Pam shuddered as if a ghost had passed through her.

"As if!" Terry looked mortified. "I wouldn't kiss her. She's blackmailing me!"

Ava thought it was time she changed the subject. "Pam, do you think we could use your computer to do an internet search?" she asked, bringing everyone back to the investigation. "We need to find out what those bird skins are worth and who might want them."

"Sure. I'm curious too." Pam sank into the seat in front of her computer screen, which was zoomed in on Terry's mask-clad face.

"They must be valuable," Tara reasoned, "else why would anyone steal them?"

Pamela typed *museum thefts*.

"You need to type in *bird skins*," Twitch told her.

"Let's see what kind of things people steal from museums first," Pam said, scrolling through the list of links. "Oooh, look, there was a Chinese jade theft a few years back. Now that I can understand. Jade is pretty. And here" – she clicked on an article – "someone stole a couple of rhino horns from a museum in Edinburgh. Rhino horns are rare now. I saw a documentary about it. They're more valuable than gold." Before Ava could read the story, Pam had already clicked away. "Check this out, gold jewellery, gemstones and antiquities stolen from the British Museum!"

"OK, but we want to know about people *buying* rare bird skins," Ava prompted. "Or who is interested in birds of paradise feathers."

Pam opened a new window and searched but was only served articles about the actual birds. "Nothing," she said. "I told you, no one in their right mind would steal—"

"Wait." Jack pointed. "Go back. There." He read out the title of an article. "'Plume Hunter Gets Plucked! Designer milliner found guilty of possessing illegal feather haul.'" He looked at Pam. "Can you print that article out?" He looked gleefully at Ava. "I'll bet any money our thief works in fashion."

"Oooh, I do hope so," Pam said enthusiastically, as the printer started to buzz.

"What's a milliner?" Terry asked.

"A hat maker," Tara replied.

"This is interesting." Ozuru had taken over the mouse and gone back to the search list.

"Victorian salmon flies," Ava read. "What are they?"

"Flies are a lure for fishing," Ozuru explained. "My dad has a friend who ties Victorian salmon flies. It's an art."

"I don't see what fishing has to do with this." Twitch skimmed the article and shook his head. "It will be a bird collector we're after, someone who wants to own Wallace's birds."

"Or will it be someone prepared to pay a lot of money for really old, rare, feathers?" Ozuru countered. "The old recipes for fly-tying need feathers from extinct birds."

"Birds of paradise aren't extinct," Twitch said.

"No, but they are protected, and you can't get hold of their feathers easily," Ozuru argued. "If it's a choice between travelling all the way to the Malay Archipelago to hunt living birds, or a trip to the Swan Museum to snatch dead ones, isn't it easier to steal birds from a museum?"

"Yes," Jack said, waving his printout. "Which is why I think we're looking for a milliner or a fashion designer."

"I've never even heard of Victorian salmon fishing ties," Ava said. Of the three theories, she thought Jack's was the most promising.

"That's because you're not into fishing," Ozuru said, sitting down at the computer and typing. "Let's see how much fly-tiers are willing to pay for feathers." A website came up: *www.classicsalmonfly.com*. "Look, there's a noticeboard."

"WHOA!" Ava was shocked by what she read. "Someone is selling a bag of six red-ruffed fruitcrow feathers for two hundred pounds!"

"From an original Victorian hat purchased at auction," Jack read. "See. Hats!"

"That makes each feather worth over thirty pounds!" Tara said.

"How many feathers are on a bird skin?" Pam asked.

They all looked at Twitch.

"On a songbird, somewhere between fifteen hundred and three thousand feathers," he replied. "But it depends on the bird. I mean, a bird of prey has over five thousand and a swan way more, something like twenty-five thousand."

"That makes one bird skin worth tens of thousands of pounds!" Terry exclaimed.

"How many did you say were stolen?" Pam's blue eyes were wide with surprise.

"Drawers and drawers of them," Ava replied. "I'd guess at least a hundred."

6

THE GAME'S A FEATHER

It was only six-thirty, but Tara's dad insisted on picking her and Ava up in his car because it was dark. Following Tara into her home, Ava removed her shoes and put them in the rack beside the door.

Ava lived in a block of flats. Her compact home was a rectangle of five brightly painted rooms, one of which was the sunny yellow bedroom she shared with her little sister. The flat was cluttered with kicked-off shoes, toys and school stuff. The walls were covered in framed photographs and Tippi's paintings. Tara's house couldn't have been more different. The clear walls were painted in earthy colours, and cream carpets or plush burgundy rugs covered the floors.

Tara led Ava into the maroon dining room. In the centre was a mahogany table laid for five. On the other side of the room was a place for prayer, with a basket containing prayer mats and, on a wooden stand, the Quran.

Dinner with the Dabiris was always a joyously chaotic affair because of Tara's younger brother, Darius, who couldn't sit still and regularly jumped off his seat to dance round the table.

Ava couldn't help but smile as she heaped her plate with saffron rice, vegetable stew, lamb and a salad of chopped cucumber, herbs and pomegranate seeds. Tara's mum always made two types of dishes because her daughter was a vegetarian. Ava knew from experience they'd both be delicious.

The girls didn't mention the museum heist at the table. Tara's father was protective, and while he approved of the birdwatching activities of the Twitchers, he was not at all happy about them chasing criminals. Ava had heard him lecture Tara several times about the dangers of playing detective and looking for trouble. Instead, Tara talked to Ava about the Twitchers' ongoing project of making and hanging fat-ball feeders around Aves Wood to help the birds through the winter months. They chatted about different recipes and humane ways of stopping cunning squirrels from stealing the bird food.

As soon as dinner was finished, the girls excused themselves and hurried up to Tara's bedroom.

Before leaving Pam's, the Twitchers had decided to visit the Swan Museum tomorrow and do a spot of investigating. The girls were eager to plan their trip.

"Tell me again about the raven," Tara said, sitting on her bed.

"After I'd climbed through the broken window" – Ava sat on the floor and stretched her legs out in front of her – "I walked towards the trees opposite. I thought the thieves might have escaped that way. But my teacher saw me and ordered me back to the coach. That's when I noticed the raven, watching me." Ava recalled the inky, unblinking stare of the bird and shivered. "It was creepy."

"People used to think witches could turn into ravens," Tara said.

"Now that's a superpower I would like to have," Ava said, reaching her arms forward and grabbing on to her toes, stretching her hamstrings.

"It's because they're fiercely clever. They can recognize and remember human faces."

"Really?" Ava sat up. She didn't know why, but she wasn't comfortable with the idea that the raven knew who she was.

"Once," Tara hugged her knees to her chest, "I saw this video of a raven solving a series of puzzles to get treats. Darius wouldn't be able to solve the puzzles that bird did."

"Clever *and* fierce. Double trouble."

"You don't think the bird robbed the museum?"

"No," Ava laughed. "Although, I can't work out how that black feather came to be in the Wallace Room."

"Are you sure it came from a raven?" Tara asked. "Or did you assume it came from a raven because you saw one outside?"

"That's a good question." Ava was unsure of the answer. Sliding the clipboard from her bag, she took out the feather and twirled it between her thumb and forefinger. "It looks like a raven feather."

"It could be a crow, or a magpie tail feather," Tara pointed out. "Would you know the difference? I wouldn't."

"No," Ava admitted. "We should've asked Twitch."

"We'll ask him tomorrow," Tara agreed. "But, it can't have been a bird that robbed the museum. For one thing, how would it carry the bird skins? In a bundle? Like a stork carrying a baby?"

Ava laughed. "Imagine if animals were raiding museums to take back their ancestors!" She found she rather liked the idea.

"It would be fair enough," Tara said, getting up. "Come on, help me get your bed out."

The two girls slid out the spare bed, stored beneath Tara's, and put on the bedding. Ava flopped onto it, looking around. Tara's room was serene. There was nothing on the pale pink walls. It had a built-in wardrobe with a dressing table on which there were some toiletries and a hairbrush. There was a desk below the window, and a row of plants on the window ledge that Tara tended faithfully as if they were her pets. Ava would've liked to be able to keep her room as neat and tidy as Tara's. It seemed to be a good place for thinking. But sharing a bedroom with Tippi made this impossible. Tippi's side of the room was chaos. The wall above her bed was plastered with drawings she was proud of. The floor was littered with clothes, dressing-up costumes and teddies. Ava had a desk on her side of the room, for homework, but it was piled with stuff. She had a poster of British birds on the spare bit of wall beside her wardrobe, above her bookshelf, which was where her binoculars, casebooks and field guides lived. On the top shelf, there was a speaker for her music. Tippi would often make her play songs from her phone and the two girls would dance madly around the room, jumping on the beds and singing at the top of their voices. She smiled, suddenly missing her boisterous sister.

"Do you think it's a good idea to let Pam come with us tomorrow?" Tara asked. "She always does exactly what she wants, no matter what she's told. She might ruin our investigation."

"I don't see that we have any choice," Ava replied. "She'll go to the museum tomorrow whether it's with us or not."

"Yes, it's better that we know where she is and what she's up to."

"I can't believe Ozuru thought Terry was her boyfriend." Ava chuckled.

"Terry was so cross." Tara's eyes danced with mirth. "But you can see why. He's such a terrible liar."

"Imagine Pam and Terry gazing into each other's eyes." Ava hooted.

"Or holding hands." Tara giggled.

"Or…" Ava snorted. "Kissing!"

"Oh stop!" Tara gasped, laughing hard. "I can't take it."

"Ozuru was so jealous…" Ava's voice was a squeak as she tried to talk through the laughing.

"Maybe *he* fancies Pam!" Tara said, and they both collapsed into fits of laughter.

"Ow!" Ava held her ribs as tears rolled down her cheeks. "It hurts!"

Ava borrowed a nightshirt from Tara and their chuckles punctuated the sounds of them getting into their nightclothes. They continued to titter as they cleaned their teeth and said goodnight to the Dabiris. But they grew serious once they'd shut the bedroom door and taken out their casebooks.

"Go over the facts," Tara said, writing *The Mystery of the Swan Museum Feather Heist* at the top of the page. "What time did you arrive?"

"Ten-thirty," Ava told her. "The doors open at ten. The robbers could've been inside already."

"Could they have broken in even earlier, through the window?"

"Not unless they're small."

"Right, sorry, go on with what you were saying."

"I gave my group the slip and went up to level five at about ten-forty-five." Ava thought for a minute. "The alarm went off, around ten-fifty, when I was looking at the bird displays. It could've been closer to eleven."

"I ran to the stairs, thinking it was a fire alarm. It must've only taken me a minute or two. Then, from the window on level four I saw people flooding out of the museum. Police cars started arriving. They came so quickly. That was when I decided to investigate…"

"You're so brave." Tara shook her head. "I would've been scared that the robbers had weapons!"

Ava blinked. The thought hadn't even crossed her mind.

"Sorry. Go on," Tara prompted.

"I spent about five or six minutes searching level four, but found nothing. Then, when I was coming down the stairs to level three, I heard this weird noise. Thinking it suspicious, I followed the sound."

"Can you describe it?" Tara asked. "What do you think it was?"

"It was a shhhhhh-ing sound like things being put into plastic bags."

"What time was this?"

"Maybe five past eleven. It's hard to tell. My heart was beating so fast it made time seem slow."

"If there was someone in the Wallace Room, stealing bird skins, then someone else had to be downstairs to trigger the alarm on the Darwin display," Tara said. "We're looking for at least two people."

"Yes…" Ava agreed. "And, the Chief Superintendent said that it looked like an amateur had tried to break into the Darwin display, that it wasn't professionals."

"That's weird." Tara scribbled this into her casebook. "The Wallace Room wasn't supposed to be open, was it?"

"No, the museum lady said it was kept locked."

"Do you think the thieves broke into the room?"

"I didn't see any damage to the door." Ava closed her eyes and pictured herself approaching it.

"Do you think they can pick locks?" Tara asked.

"No. They failed to pick the lock on the Darwin display, and the Wallace Room was locked by one of those keypads, with a number code."

"They must've had the code," Tara deduced.

"I wonder how they got it?"

"They could have someone on the inside."

"Maybe the thieves work at the museum. Write that down. That would mean the broken window was definitely a red herring or a kid from my class."

"If someone climbed out that window, there might be CCTV footage," Tara said, pleased with this thought. "We should check the locations of the cameras tomorrow."

"I hope not." Ava grimaced. "If there is, they'll have footage of me climbing through it too."

"Oops! Let's hope they don't think you're the thief."

"They won't." Ava stifled a yawn. "I'm the one who told the police to look in the Wallace Room."

"The big question is, where are the bird skins now?" Tara said. "And, if the thieves were shoving them in a plastic bag at eleven when the police were arriving, how did they get their bag of bird skins past them?" She rested her pen against her lips as she thought.

Ava yawned again and Tara snapped her casebook shut. "You need to sleep."

"I'm not tired," Ava protested.

"Yes, you are," Tara scolded, putting her casebook on her bedside table. "It seems to me that the Swan heist was planned right down to the very last second." She turned off the light. "Which means the feather thieves are very clever. If we're going to have any chance of catching them tomorrow, our brain cells need to be fully charged."

7

FEATHER UNDERWORLD

Ava's footsteps crunched on the sparkling ice that had formed across the paths overnight. Her breath rose before her like smoke. Aves Wood was under winter's spell. The morning was misty. Boughs were bare, stripped of their leaves. The once flourishing green undergrowth was shrivelled, brown and mulching. Scouring the skeletal trees for familiar landmarks, Ava felt a shiver of pleasure when she spotted the rusty old shopping trolley in the oak tree. It was the signpost to their secret headquarters. The hide was the heart and the home of the Twitchers and Ava's excitement built with every step that brought her closer to it.

As she and Tara approached, Ava saw that work had been done to maintain the camouflage of the hide, which was tricky during winter months.

"Be careful," Tara warned. "The ground may seem solid, but some of it is thin ice covering bog."

Ava heard voices. The hide door was open. She could see the tall wigwam of sticks and the hole in its roof through which a ladder climbed to a viewing platform. Beyond it was a small triangular room. Inside, a two-man tent had been erected for extra winter weather protection. Branching off the wigwam, to the left, was the cabin – originally Ozuru's dad's shed.

Inside the cabin, poring over newspapers spread across a board on two milk crates, were Jack and Twitch.

"Morning!" Jack greeted Ava and Tara cheerily. "Check out the papers."

"Mr Bettany's granddaughter, Pippa, put them aside for me when I did my paper round this morning," Twitch told them.

"The heist is on the front page of all of them." Jack pushed the *Herald* towards Ava. "They even mention the existence of a feather underworld in fashion!" His eyes were sparkling. He'd caught the scent of a motive.

"The museum says over two hundred and twenty bird skins were stolen." Twitch sounded upset.

"Two hundred and twenty!" Ava was shocked. It was dawning on her that the feather thieves had known exactly what they were doing. She wondered what kind of people planned a museum heist, uncomfortably aware that she'd almost caught them in the act.

"Something like that." Twitch nodded sadly. "It says the Swan Natural History Museum is not yet sure of the exact number of skins taken but it's estimated to be over two hundred and twenty birds from more than ten species, including: spangled cotinga, red-ruffed fruitcrow, flame bowerbird, blue chatterer, resplendent quetzal and the greater bird-of-paradise."

"This is a really big case!" Jack said, unable to hide his excitement.

"I can't imagine what two hundred and twenty birds looks like!" Tara said.

"It's more than a carrier bag of birds," Ava realized.

"Can you fit two hundred and twenty birds in a suitcase?" Tara wondered.

"I don't know." Twitch took a moment to think. "I guess they would be about the same volume and weight as two hundred and twenty assorted pairs of socks."

"Socks?" Terry said, as he and Ozuru came into the hide. "Why are we talking about socks?"

"We need two hundred and twenty of them, for an experiment," Tara told him.

"I can probably get my hands on about a hundred,"

Terry said. "There's nine of us in my house. We must all have at least ten pairs of socks, probably more."

"Do you have suitcases?" Ava asked.

"Have you met my big sisters?" Terry raised one eyebrow. "They have every size of wheelie case imaginable."

"Great," Jack said. "After we've completed our investigation of the museum, we'll go to Terry's house and perform the sock experiment."

Ozuru sat down at the table. "Have you got a plan," he said to Ava, "for how we should go about investigating the museum?"

"Me?" Ava glanced at Jack, who usually took the lead with this kind of thing, but he was looking at her expectantly.

"You're the one who discovered the crime," he said with an encouraging nod. "You were there."

"Yes." Ava stood a little taller as all eyes focused on her. "Last night, Tara and I came up with some questions that we want to answer today."

Tara pulled her casebook from her pocket. "We need to take a look at the Darwin finches display to see what it would take to set off the alarm."

"We think there has to have been at least two robbers: one to set off the decoy; one to take the bird skins," Ava explained. "We also want to find out if there is any CCTV footage of the broken window, to see if it was a route in or out of the museum before or after the crime."

"Although we think it might be a red herring," Tara added, "because it could've been broken by someone random."

"I wonder if we could persuade a security guard to let us see the footage from yesterday," Jack said.

"Doubt it," Terry replied, looking sceptical.

"Also," Ava added, "we were wondering how the robbers got the birds out of the museum with the police and security guards in the building."

"That's easy," Jack said. "The Darwin decoy made everyone think nothing had been stolen. They thought kids had been mucking about and that the museum had been evacuated. I'll bet the officers weren't being that vigilant."

Ava knew Jack was right. It was how she'd managed to investigate the broken window. She had slipped past the police so there was every possibility the thieves had too.

"I think the sock experiment is important," Tara said. "We need to know the size of the haul."

"If the bag was a big suitcase," Ava said, "it wouldn't have gone through that window."

"If two hundred and twenty balled-up socks requires a big bag, then we'll know they took the birds out a different way," Tara said. "Maybe through the front door."

"I want to talk to a curator about the missing birds," Twitch said. "We need an accurate list of what was taken. It may help us work out the motive."

"It will help us spot anyone selling them on the internet," Ozuru agreed.

"What time are we meeting Medusa at the station?" Terry asked.

"If by Medusa you mean Pam," Tara replied with a smile, "we're meeting her at eight-forty-five. The museum doesn't open till ten, the train ride is thirty-five minutes and it's a half-hour walk from the station."

"We want to be there when they open the doors," Ava said. "Before it gets busy. I'll bet loads of people will visit today, curious about the heist."

"Do we know it's definitely open?" Terry asked.

"It is," Ozuru nodded. "I checked the website this morning."

"We're not going to tell Pam the stuff we discover, are we?" Terry looked around.

"What if she discovers a clue?" Ava asked. "We'd want her to tell us, wouldn't we?"

"Ava's right. If she helps us, it's only fair we help her." Twitch gave Terry an apologetic look. "Pam is an honorary Twitcher."

"Urgh." Terry's shoulders slumped and he shot Ozuru a filthy look. "I still can't believe you thought we were a couple. For the record, I'd rather be kicked in the nuts and forced to kiss a slimy toad than be Pamela Hardacre's boyfriend."

"I'm glad to hear it." Ozuru grinned.

"I'm not sitting near her on the train," Terry declared. "None of you can make me speak to her."

"What was it that she caught you doing on camera?" Tara asked.

Ava looked at him, curious to know the answer.

"Nothing!" Terry's voice had a shrill note of panic in it. "I don't want to talk about it."

Jack took out his phone to check the time. "It's a twenty-minute walk to the station." He stuffed the newspapers into his rucksack. "We should get moving."

"I brought more fat balls for the birds." Twitch lifted a carrier bag. "We can tie them up on the way."

As they filed outside, Ava took out the black feather she'd found in the Wallace Room. "Twitch, I have a question for you." She presented the feather to him. "I think this is a raven feather, but I can't be sure. Tara made me realize I might be assuming it is because I saw a raven in the trees out the back of the museum."

"Are you sure the bird you saw was a raven?" Twitch asked, taking the feather. "It's rare to see a wild one in a town. It could've been a crow or a rook. They're all corvids."

"It was definitely a raven. It had a black beak so it couldn't have been a rook, and it was big – bigger than a crow."

"This is a tail feather, and ... yes, it belongs to a raven. First there's the length of it: crows are about the same size as pigeons; this is much longer than a pigeon feather."

Ava nodded. Twitch was an expert on all types of pigeon. He had four as pets and had trained two of them to be homing birds. He knew what he was talking about.

"Ravens have tails that are shaped like a diamond, whereas crows' are fan-shaped. You see these ends?" He grazed the arrowhead point at the end of the feather with his forefinger. "If this was a crow feather it would be blunt, or flat." He looked at her. "And then there's the colour."

"But ravens and crows are both black."

"Yes, but a raven's plumage is glossier, and while

both corvids have iridescent feathers that hint at other colours, a crow's feather has a blue or purple sheen. Ravens also have green in the mix." He rolled the feather between his thumb and forefinger and Ava saw a glimmer of green. "Raven tail feather." He handed it back to her. Ava couldn't help but be impressed.

"If ravens are rare to see in the wild, then what are the chances of this feather belonging to a different raven to the one I saw outside the museum?"

"Slim," Twitch admitted as they hurried to catch up with the others. "But why would a raven feather be in the Wallace Room?"

8

FEATHERBRAINED

"Finally!" came Pam's impatient cry as the Twitchers trooped into Briddvale Station. She was wearing a bright yellow jumpsuit, a pink faux-fur jacket and matching trainers. "I thought you were going to miss the train. Now" – she pointed to a duffel bag at her feet – "I've brought all my camera equipment so I can film interviews." She looked at them and smiled brightly. "Which one of you is going to be my cameraperson?"

"Not me," muttered Terry, stepping backwards and folding his arms. Ava quickly did the same, pulling Tara with her. Twitch and Jack stepped back a moment later.

"Ozuru! You darling. Thank you." Pam beamed and Ozuru looked baffled. "Look, the train's coming. Be a dear and carry my bag for me. It's super heavy."

Once they were settled in a carriage, Pam pulled

a wad of paper from her bag. "I found a floor plan of the museum on the website. I printed you all copies."

"This is great," Tara said as she took her map. "We can mark all of the CCTV cameras on it."

"If we shade the areas we think the cameras cover," Ava said, looking at the diagram, "we'll be able to see if there's a way in or out of the museum without being spotted."

"Brilliant," Tara nodded.

"I've made a list of the people I want to interview," Pam said, pulling a flip-top notebook from her coat pocket. "There are lots of bird curators listed on the website and they all have weird titles like 'Curator of Skin Collections' or 'Curator of Anatomical Collections', but I think the top person is a lady called Dr Trudy Nutt."

Terry sniggered at the name and Pam shot him a withering look.

"Here." She handed a page to Ava. "This is all the stuff on the website about the bird collection and the people who look after it. I couldn't find out anything about their security team, which is annoying. I definitely want to try and talk to one of them."

"Did you see?" Jack pulled the morning newspapers from his bag. "The heist is front-page news."

"No way!" Pam grabbed the papers hungrily and

scanned the articles at speed. "The police say the thieves only took the male birds! That's weird."

"Not really," Twitch said. "The male birds are the colourful ones."

"The opposite of humans then." Pam gave him a bright smile and turned back to the article. "They think the thief could either be a rare bird skin collector, a dressmaker, fashion designer or jeweller who commissioned the theft for their craft." She looked at Ava and Tara. "Remember that dress Lady Goremore wore to the Halloween Ball? That was all feathers."

Ava vividly recalled Barbara Goremore's gruesomely stylish Halloween costume. She had dressed as a bird of prey, wearing a feathered headdress dripping with rubies and a floating gown of feathers that had horrified them all.

"Don't forget fly-tiers," Ozuru said.

"It looks like there are lots of potential suspects," Jack said. "That makes things complicated because it could be one of them or an opportunist looking to sell to the highest bidder."

"Ava and I were wondering if it might be an inside job," Tara said.

"It had to be someone who knew the door code to the Wallace Room," Ava pointed out.

"I'm beginning to think it might not be a collector," Twitch said. "A collector would want both the male and female birds. By taking only the brightly coloured skins, I think we can be almost certain they were after the feathers." A pained expression crossed his face. "Which means someone is planning to cut the birds up. They may have done it already."

"Cut them up?" Tara looked aghast.

"If you're selling feathers, you're going to do it in small numbers to get the most money," Jack said.

"There's a fly-tying conference taking place this weekend up in Rookfort," Ozuru said. "I thought we might go along tomorrow and do a spot of investi—"

"I think we should find out the name of the designer who made Lady Goremore's dress," Jack said, interrupting him.

"Yes," Pam said. "I hope it is a fashion designer. That would make such a great story."

"We need to check out every possibility," Ava said, seeing Ozuru's downcast expression. "Fly-tiers have a thing for rare feathers; we saw that on their website yesterday."

Ozuru smiled gratefully at her.

"There are so many different types of suspect," Twitch said.

"How about we each investigate different leads?" Jack suggested. "Pam and I will see what we can learn about designers who use exotic feathers. Twitch can investigate collectors. Ava and Ozuru can look into the fishing thing."

"I'd like to go to the fishing conference," Tara said.

"I'll help Twitch," Terry said.

Ava nodded but couldn't help feeling dismayed. She didn't know anything about fishing and would've much rather investigated fashion designers with Jack. It sounded a lot more exciting.

They were still discussing the case when Pam jumped up shouting, "We're here!" and Swanhurst Station slid into view. She shoved the newspapers at Jack. "Ozuru, bring my bag." Bouncing over to the door as the train pulled to a stop, she pressed the button and stepped off.

"The museum is a thirty-minute walk that way." Ava pointed as they exited the station.

"Does everyone have a pound?" Pam was marching towards them. "I've spoken with a taxi driver." She waved at a people carrier. "He'll take all seven of us to the museum for seven pounds; that's a pound each."

They all nodded, taking out their money.

When they got out of the taxi, Ava checked her

watch. They they had twenty minutes before the museum doors opened. The car park was already filling up. People were curious about the robbery after hearing about it on the news.

"What shall we do till the doors open?" Terry asked, rubbing his hands and stamping his feet to keep warm.

"We could go around the outside of the building and mark the external security cameras on one of these maps," Tara suggested.

"Look." Pam glared at a van in the car park. The side door was open. A young man was sitting in it drinking from a steaming Thermos flask. "A rival news team." Ava saw the logo of a morning TV show on the van. "Ozuru and I will go and sit on the museum steps to make sure we're the first ones inside." Pam grabbed Ozuru's elbow. "Come on."

"OK," Terry said cheerfully. "Bye now." He waved at Ozuru, who was protesting weakly as he was led away.

"There are three security cameras covering this side of the building," Jack said in a low voice as they drew near. He pointed. "One, two, three."

Tara marked them on the map.

"Come this way." Ava took them round the building to the back. "There. That's the window that was broken." She pointed to the casement, which was now boarded up. The glass that had been strewn across the pathway was gone.

"Will people think we're acting suspiciously?" Terry looked about nervously. "We *are* creeping about making a note of camera locations."

"Terry, the crime already happened," Tara reminded him.

Jack marched up to the window and studied the wall and the frame. "There's no sign of damage. I don't see any marks that a crowbar might've made."

"The police said the rubber seal had been tugged out," Ava told him. "But what I couldn't work out is why the robbers let the glass fall and smash on the ground; that could draw attention."

"Maybe it was done in the dark, before the museum opened," Terry suggested.

"Then why didn't they do the robbery at night?" Jack said. "Why still be here in the morning?"

"Question is," Ava said, "were they breaking in, breaking out, or did someone unrelated break the window?"

"It's a small window," Jack said. "I'm not sure I could get through it; a grown-up definitely couldn't."

"I only just managed," Ava agreed.

Jack got down on his knees to study the flower bed.

Ava wasn't sure what he was looking for; footprints maybe. "There's nothing here," he said, dusting off his hands as he got to his feet.

"I took photos of the window yesterday, before they boarded it up," Ava said.

"Where did you see the raven?" Twitch asked her.

Ava turned and pointed across the lawn to the woods, and they headed in that direction. "It was up there, perched in the low branch of that alder tree."

"If the thief escaped out of that window," Jack said, "they might've come this way, to hide in the trees."

"That's what I thought," Ava nodded.

The gang of detectives followed the bending path that weaved between the trees, looking for clues. Jack and Ava focused on the undergrowth, Twitch searched the canopy for the raven, while Tara looked for any scrap of cloth that might've been caught on a bramble at waist height.

Terry strayed from the path, picking up the pink plastic torso of a limbless doll. "Looks to me like this place is inhabited by disturbed children…"

"Focus, Terry," Tara chided softly, but he didn't listen, moving further off into the trees.

"No way! Check this out!" Terry yelled, and they all stopped to see what he'd found. "A Transformer!

I wanted one of these so bad. My brother, Matthew, got one for his birthday and by the time he let me play with it it had no legs. You could only turn into a car crash. Hey, this one is in quite good condition. Oh, it's got no head."

Jack rolled his eyes. They carried on down the path, ignoring Terry's exclamations of delight as he worked out how to turn the robot toy into a vehicle. They had moved quite far away before they heard Terry shout, "Hey! Wait for me!"

Ava heard twigs snapping and the thud of footsteps as he ran to catch up with them, hurdling branches. There came a crunching sound. They heard Terry cry out, grunt; then a thud. Looking at each other in alarm, they hurried back along the path.

"Terry?" Tara called.

"Er, guys, I think I might've found something."

Terry was on the ground, about five metres from the path, beside a fallen tree.

"Are you all right?" Twitch asked him.

"I've hurt my ankle." Terry grimaced as he wiggled his foot. "But I think I'm OK."

"What've you found?" Ava asked.

"It's not another toy, is it?" Jack looked witheringly at the yellow robot Terry clutched in his fist.

"No." Terry pointed. "I was running to catch up with you, and as I came towards this tree trunk I slammed my foot down to hurdle over it, Ava style." He shot her a smile. "But the ground gave way and I fell, twisting my ankle. Someone has dug a big hole under here. I didn't see it because it's under the tree and covered with twigs and ivy."

They gathered around the hole. Ava took out her phone and photographed it, while Tara went around the other side of the tree.

"Do you think the thieves dug this hole to hide the bird skins here?" Terry asked hopefully.

"Maybe," Ava replied. "It's a big hole."

"Or" – Tara held up a bright red plastic spade, the kind you took to the seaside to build sandcastles – "it was dug by kids playing."

"That spade could never dig a hole like this," Twitch declared. He looked around at their blank faces. "Haven't any of you ever dug around tree roots before?" They all shook their heads. "You'd need a strong fork and a proper spade."

They looked at the red plastic thing dangling from Tara's fingers.

"So the hole could be a clue?" Terry persisted.

"Maybe." Twitch nodded.

Ava kneeled down beside Jack, who'd taken out a magnifying glass and was scanning the soil inside the hole. "It's just a big hole," he said with a shrug.

Twitch helped Terry back to the path, and they all followed it out onto the fringes of a playing field.

"Look! Ravens!" Terry pointed at a pair of black birds pecking at the frozen ground, looking for a morsel of food.

"They're crows," Twitch told him, suppressing a smile, and Ava knew with certainty that the bird she'd seen the day before had been a raven.

"The doors will be opening any minute," Twitch said, glancing at his watch.

"Let's go," Jack said.

As they passed the bus stop, Ava thought about the girl with the bruised face who'd helped her. She wished she'd got her name. The girl might've seen something that could help their investigation. A question popped into her head, and she stopped walking. What was that girl doing waiting for a bus, outside the museum, in the middle of the day? Why wasn't she at school?

Ava went into the bus stop. Getting down on all fours, she peered under the bench, seeing a lollipop stick, an old crisp packet and a greying-pink blob of bubblegum protruding from the back leg of the bench like a boil. Stuck to it was a scrunched-up ball of paper. Reaching out, she trapped the paper between her two fingers and pulled it free. Unfurling it, she caught her breath. It was a list, written in Biro.

Red-ruffed fruitcrow – *Pyroderus scutatus*
Resplendent quetzal – *Pharomachrus mocinno*
King bird-of-paradise – *Cicinnurus regius*
Magnificent riflebird – *Ptiloris magnificus*
Lovely cotinga – *Cotinga amabilis*
Spangled cotinga – *Cotinga cayana*
Purple-breasted cotinga – *Cotinga cotinga*
Superb bird-of-paradise – *Lophorina superba*
Blue bird-of-paradise – *Paradisornis rudolphi*
Flame bowerbird – *Sericulus ardens*
Greater bird-of-paradise – *Paradisaea apoda*

"Guys!" she shouted. "Come quick! I've found a definite clue!"

A NUTTY
ORNITHOLOGIST

Ava's thoughts flew to the girl who'd been sitting on the bench yesterday morning. Was this her list? Had she carelessly thrown it away? Ava remembered squeezing down behind the bench to hide from the school coach. Had the list been there then? She didn't think so. Remembering the extra police cars arriving as she'd jogged to the station, Ava wondered if the girl had panicked and got rid of the list, so there was no evidence to tie her to the robbery.

As they gathered around Ava, Jack pulled a freezer bag from his pocket and put on a pair of yellow washing-up gloves. He pointed to the list. "May I?"

Ava let him take it and watched as he carefully slid it into the freezer bag, sealing it.

"That is a list of the birds that were taken," Twitch

confirmed. "The Latin species name is written beside the common name and not all of them are birds of paradise, but they are all brightly coloured. It has to belong to the thieves."

"Get in!" Jack's face was a picture of delight. "It's our first proper clue!"

"Second," Tara reminded him. "We have the raven feather."

"Oh, yeah, the feather."

Ava could tell Jack, like the police, didn't think the feather had anything to do with the crime.

"Whoever the thieves are," Twitch said, "they aren't ornithologists, which counts against the theory of a bird collector taking the skins."

"How do you know?" Jack asked.

"Ava said the species names were written on the drawers in the Wallace Room. If the thieves need this list, telling them the names of the colourful ones, they aren't keen birdwatchers."

"Although birds are your thing," Jack pointed out. "I like birdwatching, but I've never heard of any of these birds. You don't see them around here."

"That's true," Twitch admitted, "but a collector would know them."

"The list makes it less likely it was an inside job,"

Tara said. "I mean, if someone from the museum was stealing the birds, they'd know which ones to take without writing a list."

"Only if they worked in the ornithology department," Terry said. "A geologist wouldn't necessarily know."

"If the birds were stolen to order," Jack mused, "because of the colour of their feathers, that supports my fashion designer theory."

"After the theft," Ava said, "there was a girl sitting in this bus stop. I didn't get her name. She had long black hair and a faded bruise around her eye." Ava looked at the others. "She helped me hide from the school coach, and told me how to get to the station."

"Do you think this list was hers?" Tara asked.

"I don't know," Ava admitted, realizing she didn't want the girl to be mixed up in the heist. "She probably lives around here." She waved at the houses over the field. "She was waiting for a bus."

"We should try and find her," Jack said.

"She might've seen something that could help the investigation," agreed Tara.

"I want her fingerprints. If they match the fingerprints on this" – Jack held up the list – "that's evidence that she is one of the thieves."

"I didn't see her in the museum," Ava said. "She

didn't have a bag or anything that could have carried the bird skins."

"Just because she didn't have a bag of bird skins on her doesn't mean she wasn't involved," Terry said. "Someone else could have taken them off her, or she could've hidden them somewhere … perhaps in a hole in the woods!"

"You'd hardly sit outside the museum you'd stolen from, waiting for a bus," Ava retorted, surprised by how much the accusation bothered her.

"What was she like?" Tara asked, sensing Ava's protectiveness. "Did you talk to her?"

"She was nice." Ava remembered the girl's hunched shoulders and defensive stare. "We didn't talk much. I… I felt sorry for her."

"We've got to add Bus Stop Girl to our suspect list," Twitch said apologetically, and Tara nodded.

"It's ten o'clock. The museum doors will be opening," Terry said. "C'mon, let's go and find out if the nutty professor lives up to her name."

It felt strange to Ava, to be standing in the entrance hall of the museum again.

"We can't all interview the nutty professor," Jack said.

"Don't call her that," Twitch reprimanded gently. "She's the head bird curator."

"Seven children and a video camera isn't the best way to get someone to spill sensitive information," Terry pointed out.

"I'm doing it," Pam said. "I need her take on the crime for my film."

"Film?" Ava's eyebrows lifted.

"I'm making a documentary," Pam declared.

"I think Twitch should do it," Tara said. "He'll understand what Dr Nutt's saying about the bird skins. He's the only one of us who knows about birds of paradise."

"Fine, so me and Twitch—" Pam started to say.

"I think Ava should go with Twitch," Jack said. "Of all of us, she's most likely to be able to get Dr Nutt to talk to her, because she discovered the crime."

"But…" Pam tried to interject.

"Pam." Jack turned to her. "You and Ozuru need to find the head of security. It's vital we get to see the CCTV footage from yesterday morning. The police will already have it. We need it too."

"But I want to interview the curator." Pam pouted.

"Let her interview the nutty professor," Terry said, "'cause there's no way she's going to persuade a security guard to let her see top-secret CCTV tapes." He chuckled. "Not with her lack of charm."

"Oh yeah?" Pam's hands went to her hips as she spun around to glare at Terry. "I could too!"

"Sure you could." Terry gave her a maddening grin.

"It's all right, Pam," Tara said sweetly. "There's no shame in not being able to do something."

"What?" Pam looked at Tara as if she were talking gibberish.

"Maybe it should be me that talks to security," Jack said. "You know, man to man."

"You're not a man!" Pam grabbed Ozuru's arm. "Come on, Ozuru. We'll show them." As she marched him away, Pam looked over her shoulder and scowled at them. "I'll get that footage, just you see if I don't."

"She's a formidable weapon if you point her in the right direction," Terry said, looking pleased with himself.

"You totally played her!" Ava said, impressed.

"Reverse psychology." Terry nodded. "It works every time. My sisters taught me that."

"I feel sorry for the security guard." Tara giggled.

"Right." Jack rubbed his hands together. "Twitch and Ava are going to find the bird curator. That leaves us" – he nodded at Terry and Tara – "to take a close look at the case of Darwin's finches and, if possible, a peek at the crime scene."

"See you in a bit," Tara said to Ava as the group split up.

"Meet you at the picnic tables," Jack called after them.

"I think the curator's offices might be on level five," Ava said, thinking of the NO PUBLIC ACCESS sign she'd seen yesterday.

When the lift doors opened, Ava headed straight for the corridor, then realized Twitch was gone from her side. She glanced back and saw him standing before the birds of paradise display.

"Have you got your phone?" Twitch asked as she came back. "The camera is rubbish on mine."

"Sure," she said, handing it over. "Why?"

"I want a close-up picture of each of the specimens on that list you found. For reference, so everyone knows what the birds look like. That way we'll all know what we're looking for. These are the Birds of the World." He gestured to the gallery. "They'll all be here somewhere."

"But Jack's got the list."

"I know what was on it."

"You remember all the birds on the list?"

"Course." Twitch snapped a picture. "That's how I know the thief wasn't an ornithologist. And I don't think they care about Alfred Russel Wallace either. Not all the birds in those drawers will have been collected by him. I know it's called the Wallace Room, but a museum stores by species not by collector. This was a feather smash and grab for money. They don't care if they're destroying history."

Leaving Twitch taking pictures, Ava crept down the dark wood-panelled corridor. There were doors spaced along it with brass plaques at waist height. Names were engraved on them. The third one on the left said Dr T. Nutt.

"Twitch," she called out in a hushed voice. "I've found her."

"She might not work on a Saturday," Twitch said, coming to stand beside Ava as she knocked.

"Come in," came a familiar gravelly voice.

Ava glanced at Twitch, suddenly nervous. Neither of them opened the door, and then it opened by itself.

"Can I help… Oh! It's you!" Dr Trudy Nutt was no longer wearing a toffee-coloured suit, but was dressed in jeans and a floral shirt. "Come in."

She stepped back and Ava saw she wasn't wearing shoes. Her dark hair, which had been pinned up yesterday, was now a Catherine wheel of wisps around her face, held back by a pair of thick-framed glasses.

There were dark shadows under her eyes.

Ava followed Twitch into the room and closed the door. A gold-framed painting of flamingos hung between two windows. The rest of the walls were lined with books. In the middle of the room stood a desk of polished wood on a threadbare rug.

"Er, hello, Dr Nutt," Ava said, haltingly.

"You're the girl who discovered the theft aren't you? What's your name?"

Ava's throat was suddenly dry.

"Her name is Ava Kingfisher," Twitch said, offering his hand. "I'm Corvus Featherstone. We're members of a birdwatching detective society called the Twitchers. We wanted to talk to you about the theft."

"I want to talk to you," Dr Trudy Nutt said, directing them to sit on a green chaise longue. She wheeled her chair out from behind her desk, sitting opposite, looking eagerly at Ava. "When you said you'd discovered the bird skins were gone, I didn't want to believe you. I was so relieved the Darwin finches were safe…" She trailed off.

"Do you have a theory as to who might have stolen the birds?" Twitch asked.

"A theory?"

"Yes. We've considered the species that were taken:

all male birds, all colourful species, not all necessarily rare, and am I right that they weren't all Wallace's birds?"

Dr Trudy Nutt nodded, looking startled by Twitch's knowledge.

"Then, I believe the skins were stolen to order, for the feathers." He sighed. "I had thought it might be a collector after Wallace's skins."

"If it was a collector," Dr Trudy Nutt said, "then there would at least be a chance we'd get the bird skins back intact. But I fear you are right."

"Do you think the feathers were taken to make hats or dresses?" Ava asked.

"That's what the police suspect. Either fashion or there are a couple of taxidermists who've been charged with this kind of crime."

"Taxidermists?" Twitch echoed.

"Yes, there's quite a community of people who stuff skins. They have customers who would pay a high price for a stuffed and mounted Wallace bird of paradise." She looked downcast. "The police are also investigating the possibility of it being an inside job. That's why I'm so relieved to see you." She smiled at Ava.

"Me?"

"Yes. The police want to talk to you," Dr Nutt said.

A spark of fear fizzed in Ava's chest.

"Don't look alarmed. They just want you to give a statement, telling them what you saw. You're the only witness to the crime and we didn't even have your name. I'm so glad you came."

"I didn't *see* the actual crime," Ava said hurriedly. She'd come here looking for answers, not to be asked questions.

"I am hoping your statement might shed some light on things. If you could see how upset and demoralized the staff here are over the loss of those birds, you'd know it couldn't have been an inside job."

"Why do the police think it's an inside job?" Twitch asked.

"The number lock on the door of the Wallace Room – it's only known to staff."

"Is it changed regularly?" Ava asked.

"Perhaps not regularly enough. The door codes are changed every three months." Dr Nutt shook her head and her glasses fell into her lap. "We need to find those birds before they're … dismantled." This last word came out in a ghastly whisper. "The moment their labels are removed, they'll be lost to science."

"Labels?" Ava asked.

"Each skin has a label detailing the date the skin was collected, the location, and by whom. We must recover the skins with their biodata labels to be able to re-enter them into the collection. With such a large number of this type of bird gone, there is a big hole in our scientific record of the species."

"Is that bad?" Ava asked.

"The birds here are part of the most important collection in the world. The museum has over a million specimens which covers nearly ninety-five per cent of all the Earth's known species of bird. Each of those birds has taken many man-hours to find, catch, collect, preserve and label. Some are two hundred years old. Its value is incalculable."

"That's a lot of dead birds," Ava frowned. "I don't understand why museums need to collect them."

"Collections demonstrate what life we have on this planet, but they also show us what we've lost, or may lose in the future. They are the conscience of the world. They guide our behaviour." She looked at Ava. "To understand what is happening as bird populations move and change, to have a hope of learning why, we need to know how they behaved in the past. This is becoming increasingly important during this time of climate change."

"They can help you work out what might happen in the future?" Ava found this marvellous.

"Yes. Researchers from across the globe use our collection to learn about evolution, genomics, ecology, archaeology, anatomy, taxonomy and more." She pressed her fingers into the corners of her eyes, then put her glasses back on. "You cannot put a price on a collection. It isn't about money; it's about knowledge. Those missing birds won't be available to future generations of scientists. We can't know the damage … the *cost* to humankind." She exhaled with her whole being. "As the senior curator in charge of the birds under this roof, it breaks my heart that this has happened on my watch…" She pressed her lips together and Ava wondered if she were about to cry. "If you children know anything that could help find those birds, please, you must tell me. I must get them back."

"We want to help," Ava assured her. "That's why we're here."

"How was it that you came to discover the theft?" Dr Nutt's hazel eyes rested on Ava.

"I was here on a school trip," Ava told her. "I was on this floor when the alarm went off. When I got down to level three, I heard a weird noise. I followed it to the Wallace Room. The door was ajar. I peeped in. There was no one there. I… I…" Ava glanced guiltily at Dr Nutt. "I was curious about what was in the cupboards. I opened one, but it was empty. Then I heard you talking to that police officer." Ava knew what she was saying might get her in trouble, but she wanted to tell the truth. "I didn't come out of the Wallace Room because I was scared. I stayed in there until you went away. That's when I saw the raven feather on the floor."

"A raven feather?" Dr Nutt sat bolt upright. "How odd! On my way into work yesterday, George – our head of security who mans the staff entrance – quoted Shakespeare's play *Macbeth* at me. He said, 'The raven himself is hoarse, that croaks the fatal entrance of Duncan, under my battlements.'" She looked at Ava. "Why do you think he did that?"

"Because he'd seen a raven," Ava gasped.

10
CLEVER AS A CROW

Ava shuddered at the cold as she and Twitch walked across the grass to the picnic tables, where Terry, Jack and Tara were waiting for them. They'd spent nearly an hour talking to Dr Trudy Nutt. As she and Twitch sat down with Jack, Ozuru and Pam emerged from a side door that said PRIVATE ACCESS.

"Here comes trouble," Terry muttered.

"Pam is a genius," Ozuru declared, hurrying over with the camera in his hands and the empty bag bopping against his thigh.

"I wouldn't say that," Pam said, looking like the cat that got the cream.

"You should have seen her interviewing George, the security guard," Ozuru gushed.

Pam turned to Terry. "Ask me if I saw the CCTV camera footage." She looked down at her brightly polished nails, admiringly. "Go on, ask me."

"Nah," Terry replied. "Not really that interested."

"She did! She got it!" Ozuru blurted out. "Tell them, Pam."

"Well…" Pam parted Terry and Tara to sit in the middle. "We asked where we could find the head of security and Flossie, the girl at the ticket counter, told us his name was George and where the security office was."

"She did it in exchange for a selfie with Pam and the chance to spotlight on her channel," Ozuru told them.

Ava blinked. She hadn't realized anyone watched Pam's channel.

"All right, Ozzie, I'm telling the story," Pam chided.

"Ozzie?" One of Terry's eyebrows lifted.

"It's my little nickname for him, isn't it, Ozzie?"

Ozuru blushed.

"Anyway, when we got to the staff entrance, which is that door we came out of," Pam said, "I made a huge fuss about wanting to interview George." She clapped her hand over her heart. "And, guys, he is such a cute old man! He invited us into his office and made me a cup of tea with a biscuit."

"Pam told him she was making a documentary on the unsung heroes working at the museum," Ozuru butted in, "and that she wanted him to be the star of her film."

Pam held up a hand, indicating Ozuru should let her speak. "George showed us a big monitor, sliced into squares. It shows the feeds from all the CCTV cameras around the building." She held up her phone. "I took a picture of it, so we can work out which camera feed comes through to each square of the screen." She paused for them to acknowledge her brilliance.

Jack was so impressed his mouth opened but no words came out.

"That's nothing. Go on," Ozuru prompted Pam. "Tell them what you did next."

"I said that I'd heard about the awful robbery, and that I expected he was working closely with the police to catch the evil thieves, and he said yes, he was. I asked if he'd had to give them a copy of the CCTV footage and when he said yes, I asked how he'd done it, seeing as everything was digital now and computers were so complicated." Pam put her finger to her lip and tipped her head, as if she were ditsy, then laughed. "Lovely George pointed at a video file sitting on his desktop computer and said it was the feed from the security cameras from yesterday morning. I asked him if he'd seen anything suspicious. He said that he hadn't and that there was nothing on camera that gave a clue to the identity of the thieves. Then I came up with the bright idea of interviewing him with the CCTV footage from the morning of the theft playing in the background, for the added drama."

"He said yes!" Ozuru crowed. "I set up the camera to point directly at the big screen and whilst Pam was positioning his chair, she got him to open the CCTV file. It was password-protected and everything."

"I asked George to start the footage at 10.30am and then I interviewed him for as long as possible, which was sooooo hard because he's really boring, but we've got at least three quarters of an hour of the footage."

"That definitely covers the time of the theft," Ava said, becoming excited.

"OK," Terry said begrudgingly. "That *is* clever."

"Dr Trudy Nutt said George talked about a raven when she arrived yesterday," Twitch said to Pam. "Did he mention the bird at all?"

"Yes!" Ozuru exclaimed. "He did. One of the squares, where there should be a camera feed, was black. I asked why and George said that early yesterday morning a raven had pecked at the camera until it broke!"

"Whoa!" Jack looked at Ava. "Your hunch about that bird having something to do with the theft might be right!"

"Come on then." Terry looked at Twitch. "Hit us with your raven knowledge."

"What makes you think I know anything about ravens?" Twitch grinned.

"I don't know, *Corvus*," Jack said, using Twitch's given name. "Maybe it's something to do with your superhero alter-ego, Bird Boy."

"OK, listen up, bird fans," Twitch said. "Ravens are corvids, members of the crow family. Corvids are clever … cunning even. Their intelligence is legendary. Clever corvids can be found in old myths and stories. There are debates about which is cleverer, the raven or the crow, but both have the problem-solving abilities of a seven-year-old human. Ravens are the biggest corvid. They can have a wingspan of up to one hundred and fifty centimetres. They eat all sorts of stuff: carrion, small mammals, other birds or their eggs."

"They eat other birds?" Terry grimaced.

"Two ravens can trap, kill and strip a pigeon of its flesh in minutes," Twitch replied.

"Oh!" Tara looked horrified.

"They are a bird to treat with respect," Twitch said. "If they're angry with you, they'll hurt you. They remember human faces and are known to hold grudges."

Ava wondered if the bird she'd seen in the alder tree remembered her.

"Right, so, don't annoy a raven," Terry said. "Got it."

"Did Dr Nutt tell you anything else useful?" Jack asked.

"The police think it might be an inside job," Ava replied. "She also said the police think it's most likely the feathers were stolen for a fashion designer or, possibly, a taxidermist."

"A taxidermist? Why?" Tara asked.

"To stuff the skins and sell the rare Wallace birds to rich people," Twitch said.

"George doesn't think it was an inside job," Pam said. "I asked him."

"No, Dr Nutt doesn't think it is either," Ava said.

"Well, we" – Jack pointed his pen at Terry and Tara – "couldn't get into the Wallace Room. The door is locked and there's yellow tape criss-crossing it declaring it to be a crime scene. However, we did notice there is a small window opposite the door which lets light into the corridor. It might be possible, if you had a camera on a really long stick, to be able to film someone punching the door code into the keypad." He paused, looking round, but it was obvious from everyone's silence and sceptical expressions that no one thought this was likely. "Yeah, I know, it's a long shot." He shrugged. "Just thought it was worth saying."

"We had better luck with the Darwin exhibit

though," Tara said. "There were loads of people who wanted to see it, because the newspapers said a break-in was attempted. A security guard was standing beside it."

"The case is enormous," Terry said. "At least two metres tall. You can see the big crack clearly."

"But it's weird," Jack said. "The crack isn't where you'd think it would be. It's in the top of the case."

"Only an idiot would lob a stone onto the roof of a case to try and smash it open," Terry said.

"That doesn't make sense," Twitch said, frowning.

"Exactly." Terry waggled his eyebrows. "We took photos of the crack, obviously."

"So, to recap," Jack said, looking down at his casebook where he'd been scribbling notes. "We've got the appearance of a mysterious raven that took out a CCTV camera. Ava found a shopping list for the stolen bird skins in the bus stop where she met a weird girl with a bruised face. The police suspect it's an inside job or possibly a taxidermist. Pam has filmed the CCTV footage from the time of the crime." He looked around at them. "Did I miss anything?"

"There is one more thing," Ava said, feeling dread like a cold leech sucking at her stomach. "I've got to go to the police station and give a statement. Dr Nutt says they're looking for me."

11

STATEMENT
FOR STICKLER

"You mustn't worry," Tara said, linking her arm through Ava's as they set off for the police station. "We're all coming with you."

"They won't let you into the interrogation room," Ava replied with a wince of a smile. She didn't want to admit that she was scared about giving her witness statement. She thought back to the last time she'd been in a police station interrogation room and it made her clench her teeth. A female officer had been firing question after question at her about her mum. Ava had been so scared of saying the wrong thing that she had shut down completely and said nothing. The officer eventually told her that her silence wasn't helping her mum's case. Ava had been terrified. She hadn't understood what was happening. Nan had brought in a solicitor who'd told Ava she'd done the right thing, but she'd always wondered: if she'd answered the officer's questions, would things have turned out differently for her mum?

"It's this way," Ozuru said, consulting the map on his phone and directing them.

Ten minutes later, the seven of them were standing outside Swanhurst Police Station.

Jack opened the door and marched up to the window in the counter as the others filed in behind him. "Good afternoon," he said to the officer at the desk. "We need to speak to the Chief Superintendent."

The officer's eyebrows lifted. "I'm afraid Chief Superintendent Stickler is busy."

Ava came forward. "My name is Ava Kingfisher," she said. "I was the girl at the Swan Museum yesterday who told Chief Superintendent Stickler about the missing bird skins. Dr Trudy Nutt says he's looking for me to give a witness statement."

"Oh! Yes!" The officer was suddenly alert. "Don't go anywhere. I won't be a moment." She hurried away.

Ava felt like there was an invisible belt tightening around her ribs, stopping her from breathing freely.

"We're not going anywhere," Jack reassured her. "We're going to sit here" – he waved a hand at the waiting room chairs – "until you're done. And if it takes too long" – he smiled – "we'll set Pam on them."

Ava tried to smile back.

Pam was whispering loudly to Ozuru, telling him to film Ava. Ozuru was shaking his head.

"Just think about what Dr Nutt said," Twitch told her. "We've got to get those birds back to the collection with their labels. Your statement could help make that happen."

"I know." Ava held out her hand. "Jack, I need the list. I'm going to have to give them our clues."

"I didn't get a chance to dust it for fingerprints," he said mournfully, as he reluctantly handed her the freezer bag with the list inside.

The desk officer returned and unlocked a hatch in the counter. "Come through," she said to Ava.

"We'll be here waiting for you," Tara said, getting up and placing a reassuring hand on Ava's arm.

Pam grabbed the camera from Ozuru and hit record. "The brave Ava Kingfisher is going into the police station to give a witness statement," she said. "She's going to tell Chief Superintendent Stickler about how she discovered the missing birds in the Wallace Room at the Swan Museum." She turned the camera on herself and moved to stand in front of the others. "I'm Pamela Hardacre, here with the Twitchers at Swanhurst Police Station. They are investigating the Swan Museum Heist..."

"No filming inside the station," the officer barked.

"What are you doing?" Terry hissed as Pam let the camera drop.

"I'm letting the officer know that Ava's to be treated nicely," Pam replied in a clear loud voice, "unless she wants to end up on YouTube."

Ava flung Pam a grateful smile.

The officer led Ava through a nondescript corridor to an empty room containing a table, chairs and a box of tissues. "Chief Superintendent Stickler won't be long," the officer said and she shut the door.

Ava's heart thudded an odd rhythm as she tried to control her bursts of fear. It was almost a relief when the door finally opened and the Chief Superintendent came in. He was accompanied by a younger, smiling, female officer.

"Hello again," Chief Superintendent Stickler said, pulling out a chair and sitting down opposite Ava. "I'm told Dr Nutt sent you to give a witness statement. Good, good."

Ava wanted to point out that nobody had sent her; she'd come of her own accord. But she knew better than to quarrel with a police officer. Instead, she nodded.

The female officer had a tablet in her hands. She laid it on the table and Ava saw it was recording their conversation.

"Let the record show that it is" – Chief Superintendent Stickler looked at his watch – "two-twenty-three p.m. on the eleventh of February. I, Chief Superintendent Mark Stickler, am here with Officer Stacy Beaumont, taking the witness statement of Ava Kingfisher concerning the robbery on the tenth of February at the Swan Museum."

Ava swallowed.

"Now…" Chief Superintendent Stickler brought his hands together, steepling his fingers as he reclined in his chair. "Why don't you tell us, in your own words, everything you saw from the moment you arrived at the museum yesterday morning."

Ava launched into her story of how she discovered the missing birds. She paused, wondering if she should admit to sneaking back into the museum to investigate the broken window and seeing the raven in the woods.

"That's very helpful, thank you," Chief Superintendent Stickler said, assuming she'd finished. He looked at Officer Beaumont. "Do you have any questions for Miss Kingfisher?"

"No." Officer Beaumont sat up a little straighter. "Her story matches what we already know."

112

"Well, I will say this, Miss Kingfisher." Chief Superintendent Stickler gave Ava a stern look. "The next time you are in a building and an alarm goes off, don't be so foolish as to stay inside. If there had been a fire, you could've been killed."

"I'm sorry," Ava replied, bristling. She couldn't help thinking he should be thanking her. If she hadn't told him about the Wallace Room, he wouldn't have discovered the theft for a lot longer. "I won't do it again."

"I think we're all done here." Chief Superintendent Stickler rolled his right shoulder back, as if a muscle was bothering him, and his neck clicked loudly.

"Don't you want to know my theory about the crime?" Ava asked.

"I think you've been very detailed in the statement you've given us," he replied, barely looking at her.

"But … but, I hadn't finished. I've got two clues for you." Ava hurriedly withdrew the black feather from her bag, then tugged the freezer bag containing the crumpled list of birds from her pocket. "This is the feather I found on the floor in the Wallace Room. It's from a raven." She laid it on the table. "And this note…" She held it up so he could see it clearly. "I found this stuck to bubblegum underneath the bus stop bench at the museum. It's a list of the birds that were stolen."

Ava found she was reluctant to tell him about the girl in the bus stop. "Perhaps someone involved in the crime caught a bus afterwards…"

"You've been very helpful, Miss, er, Kingfisher," Chief Superintendent Stickler said. Officer Beaumont reached for the feather and the note, but he lifted his hand. She immediately retracted hers. "You can keep your" – he paused – "clues. We'll be in touch if we need them."

"Don't you even want to look at this list?" Ava placed it in front of him. "My theory is that the thieves might've used it as reference when taking the bird skins. It could have fingerprints on it."

Chief Superintendent Stickler glanced at it and sighed. "It looks exactly like the list of birds on our press release, which was printed in the newspapers today." He stood up. "Thanks for coming in. We will be in touch if we need to talk to you again."

Ava stared at the Chief Superintendent in disbelief as he left the room.

"The sergeant on desk duty will be in in a minute to take down your contact details and then you're free to go," Officer Beaumont explained with an apologetic smile, before hurrying after the Chief Superintendent.

"I'll get Miss Kingfisher's statement transcribed

for the case file," Officer Beaumont was saying as the door closed.

A rebellious flame ignited in Ava's chest. Silently, she got up and ran to the door, pressing her ear against it. She heard Chief Superintendent Stickler saying, "I can't stand it when kids think they're detectives." His words felt like a slap. "I ask you, a black feather and a note in a bus stop?" He snorted. "She probably wrote it herself. I've been in this game long enough to know that this is either an inside job, or it's a targeted hit by one of the antiquity gangs."

12

SOCK IT TO THEM

On the train home, there was great debate about what had happened at the police station.

"It was so rude." Ava was still angry with Chief Superintendent Stickler for what he'd said about kids being detectives.

"But on the bright side," Tara said, "we've still got our clues."

"And we know the police think it's either an insider or a gang of antiquity thieves." Jack looked thrilled that a gang might be involved. "That was a good bit of sleuthing you did there."

"I can't believe there are gangs out there that target museums." Twitch looked out of the window thoughtfully. "They must be awful people."

"The police not listening to you," Pam said to Ava, "is great for my film."

"Why?" Ozuru asked.

"Well, you lot are the underdogs, right?" Pam looked round at them. "Don't look at me like that, of course you are. You don't have the manpower, the experience, or the resources of the police. You're kids!"

"So?" Jack lifted his chin and narrowed his eyes.

"So you tried to help them, and they laughed in your face…"

"Thanks for explaining it." Ava snorted.

"But if you solve the case, it'll be David beating Goliath, won't it? The underdog biting the butt of the bulldog! Viewers love that sort of thing. It'll be a huge story." Pam paused. "Of course, you'll have to solve the case first."

"Oh, don't you worry. We will," Ava said forcefully, looking at Jack who was nodding. There was nothing she wanted more than to see the surprised look on Chief Superintendent Stickler's face when they solved the case and returned the birds to the museum.

"I'll dust for fingerprints tonight." Jack waved the freezer bag with the list inside triumphantly.

"Aw, cute!" Pam said. "You have a toy fingerprint kit."

"It's not a toy," Jack told her. "It's a real kit with different pots of powder and an FBI manual on how to professionally lift prints off different surfaces. And there are cards, so you can keep a record of people's prints."

"We still need to figure out how big the bag would need to be to fit two hundred and twenty birds," Tara reminded them.

"My guess is it's the same size as the hole I fell in," Terry said.

"That hole could've been dug for any number of reasons," Tara replied.

"Tara's right," Ava said. "Until we know how big two hundred and twenty birds is, we won't be able to work out how the thieves got them out of the museum, or know if they were hidden in that hole."

"It's nearly four o'clock," Terry said. "Why don't we go to my house now and find out what a hundred socks looks like? Tomorrow, I have Mass in the morning, then Sunday lunch. It'll be much harder to sneak around the house stealing everyone's socks."

"What about the CCTV camera footage?" Pam said. "Shouldn't we go back to mine and watch it?"

"Is there a way we can do both?" Twitch asked.

Terry thought. "My brother's supposed to be coming home from university this afternoon," he said. "He might let us borrow his laptop to watch it."

"Great," Jack said. "We'll watch the CCTV footage while we're collecting socks."

* * *

Ava liked Terry's house. The front door was rarely locked during the day and there was always someone in the kitchen making a sandwich or a drink. Terry had three brothers and three sisters who often brought friends home. Terry's parents were so used to the tides of young people ebbing and flowing through the place that they called everyone "mate" and never asked awkward questions. The walls of the Vallis residence reverberated with friendly teasing and cheerful bickering and everyone was welcome.

They trooped up the stairs to Terry's bedroom, which he shared with his fifteen-year-old brother Matthew. It contained two unmade beds and the floor was carpeted with clothes. As he entered, Terry kicked the clothes over to his brother's side of the room. "I'll go get a suitcase from on top of Louise's wardrobe." He nodded to a chest of drawers beside his bed. "There are socks in there, and in that one over there. Who wants to get them out?"

"We will, won't we, Ava?" Tara volunteered and Ava nodded.

"Ozuru, come with me." Terry picked up a black bin bag from the floor, opened it and recoiled from the smell. He tipped it upside down over an overflowing laundry basket in the corner of the room. A damp mouldering PE kit dropped out. "Ozuru…" He shoved the empty bin bag into his hands. "You know where my parents' room is. You can raid their drawers for socks and put them in here."

Ozuru looked unhappy with this plan.

"Where's that laptop?" Pam asked, hugging her hands around her chest, looking nervous about touching anything.

"Luke's room is next door. Be sure to knock and ask nicely."

"I can be nice," Pam said, backing out of the room.

"Where do you want me and Twitch to sock hunt?" Jack asked.

"The laundry room down by the kitchen. There's bound to be tons of clean socks on the drying rails."

Everyone disappeared, leaving Tara and Ava alone in the bedroom. Tara wrinkled her nose, straightened Terry's duvet and sat down on the edge of the bed. "It smells of boys in here."

"Is that what that smell is?" Ava grimaced and they both laughed.

"Oh! I have an idea." Tara ran out of the room, crossed the landing to the bathroom and returned pulling on a pair of rubber gloves.

"Smart thinking."

"You empty the drawers of the clean socks," Tara said. "I'll fish for the dirty ones." And she went at the clothes on the floor like a combine harvester, grabbing and hurling anything that wasn't a sock into a mound in the corner. The socks she found she put on Matthew's bed. Ava opened each drawer retrieving every sock she spotted.

"Luke's much better looking than Terry," Pam said, returning with a silver laptop and a charger cable. "Did you know he's studying classics at university?" She opened the laptop and plugged it in. "He told me his password, but I can't tell it to you. I promised to keep it a secret."

Curious, Ava looked over Pam's shoulder as she plugged her camera into the laptop. The video file opened. The only bit of the security guard Ozuru had filmed was his ear and hair at the edge of the picture. The rest of the frame was taken up with nine squares, eight of them a feed from a museum CCTV camera, one of them black. Pam switched the sound off, so they didn't have to listen to George.

"It's so clever, the way you got this footage," Ava told Pam and she was surprised by how pleased Pam seemed at the praise.

"Thanks," Pam smiled. "Now let's see if there are any clues to be had from it."

Terry returned with a huge canvas suitcase. He lay it in the space on the floor that Tara had cleared. He and Tara started counting balled-up socks into it, while Pam and Ava watched the screen.

"Got your parents' socks," said Ozuru, coming in clutching the black bag. Jack and Twitch came in behind him with a laundry basket half full of socks.

Ava barely glanced at them. Her eyes were fixed on the screen.

"There'll be more in my sisters' rooms," Terry told Ozuru, then he looked at Jack and pointed across the landing. "That's Peter's room. He's at work. Go into his wardrobe. There's three drawers inside. Top one is pants. Second one is socks."

"Seventeen, eighteen, nineteen…" Tara counted. When she reached twenty, she paused to mark it down in her casebook. Then she started again. "One, two, three…"

When the Vallis house had been scoured for socks, and they'd all been counted into the suitcase, it contained one hundred and ninety-seven pairs.

"It's only two thirds full," Terry observed, zipping it shut. "I mean, you could fit another twenty pairs of socks in that suitcase and close it, no problem."

Jack lifted the suitcase. "It's not very heavy."

"You could probably cram two hundred and twenty bird skins into a smaller suitcase than this, but you'd risk crushing them," Tara said.

"If you were stealing the bird skins because the feathers were worth money, you wouldn't want to damage them," Jack said. "You'd want to wrap each one in tissue paper or something."

"You might not have time," Terry said.

"If it's a gang of thieves, they could've split the birds between four rucksacks and walked out the front door," Twitch said.

"Both the insider theory and the gang theory mean that the smashed window is a red herring," Jack said.

"Except," Ava said, noticing something about the CCTV footage, "the camera that the raven broke is the one covering that window."

"Terry," Ozuru said, opening up the suitcase and staring at the mound of paired socks. "How are we going to know whose socks are whose and which ones are clean? They're all jumbled up!"

"Err." Terry blinked. "I can probably pick out my own…"

"Sniff test?" Jack suggested.

"Oh!" Tara recoiled.

"That'll take too long." Terry thought for a moment.

"I know, we'll stuff the socks into any old drawer and let my brothers and sisters work it out for themselves. I'll say it's an April Fool's joke."

"It's February," Twitch said.

"A prank then," Terry said. "I'll say it was Matthew's idea."

Suddenly Ava glimpsed a familiar figure over Pam's shoulder. "That's her!" she cried. "That's the girl from the bus stop, in the middle square." Pam's hand went to the space bar, to pause it. "No, let it play."

Ava watched as the girl from the bus stop filed into the museum entrance with her classmates; her black clothes blending in with their black-and-purple uniforms. So, she had been in the museum at the time of the robbery! But she wasn't carrying a bag.

A series of separate thoughts in Ava's head were magnetically drawn to one another, creating a sequence. Drawing in a sharp breath, Ava grabbed a pair of socks from the suitcase, took the empty bin liner from Ozuru and dropped them in. It made a familiar sound.

"Oh! I think I know how she did it!"

13

THE IMPROBABLE TRUTH

Everyone looked at Ava.

"You think you know how who did what?" Jack asked.

Ava didn't reply. Instead she turned to Twitch. "Is it possible to train a raven?"

"I guess," he replied hesitantly, "but birds are not like dogs. They don't always do as they're told."

"What if" – Ava felt a thrill of excitement as the theory came together in her head – "there is no gang or insider, and the robbery was committed by a girl and her raven?"

"How?" Tara asked.

"I'll explain," Ava said, turning to the suitcase. "But first, help me put the socks in this bin bag."

Six pairs of hands grabbed the balled-up socks and flung them into the bag. Pam watched with a wrinkled nose.

"Stop." Ava halted them as the bag filled up. "We need a second bin bag."

Terry zoomed out of the room, clattered down the stairs, a cupboard door slammed, then Ava heard the thud of his feet as he returned and burst back into the room.

She took the second bin bag, opened it, and decanted the remaining socks into it. "Pam, have you got one of those maps of the museum you printed out?"

Pam was setting up her camera on a shelf. She pressed record, before pulling a map from her bag.

"See if you can find a route from the Wallace Room down to the toilet with the broken window that doesn't take you down the main staircase."

"I'd take the lift," Pam said, without looking at the map.

"Of course!" Jack's head snapped up. "No one would be using the lifts while the alarm was going off, in case of a fire!"

"OK, so…" Ava held up her hands. "Bus Stop Girl had the whole thing planned out. She knows that Friday is school visit day; that's why the robbery happened then. The first thing that happens is her raven takes out the CCTV camera that covers the toilet window. She sits in the bus stop, waiting for the first school coach to arrive."

"Thank goodness it was yours," Jack muttered.

"Bus Stop Girl merges with the kids entering the museum. Once inside, she goes to the Darwin display, inserting a metal rod into the lock and placing a stone on the ground beside it. Meanwhile, her raven is pulling the rubber seal from the window. The glass falls out and smashes. The bird flies in, up the corridor, and into the Creatures That Made History exhibition on the ground floor, where she's waiting for him. She shows him the stone. It must be a stone the bird knows or has trained with. Then, she and the raven go up to level three, to the Wallace Room."

"Don't you think a girl and a raven would draw attention?" Terry said.

"My class wouldn't notice if someone in a clown suit jumped out in front of them," Ava replied, "and there was hardly anyone else in the museum. It was early. Plus, she was wearing black. If she had the bird under her arm, held against her chest the way that Twitch holds his chickens, I don't think people would have noticed. Anyway, she took the lift. I'm certain of it because I remember, before I got in, I had to call the lift from level three."

Ava paused to gather her thoughts. "So, Bus Stop Girl goes up to level three with her raven, to the Wallace Room."

"But it's locked," Tara said.

"Yes," Ava looked at Jack. "But you said there is a small window opposite the door."

"There is."

"What if, when she was planning the robbery, the girl had sent the bird up to the window to watch people when they keyed the code into the door. What if the bird had learned the key?" She looked at Twitch. "Is that possible?"

"It's possible," Twitch said, sounding sceptical.

"The raven keys the code into the lock and opens the Wallace Room door?" Pam asked.

"Yes. They go inside. We know the bird must've been with her because we found the feather."

"I guess." The expression on Pam's face showed she wasn't convinced.

"Bus Stop Girl has folded bin bags in her pocket," Ava continued. "She takes out one and, using her list, she finds the birds and puts them in the bag. The sound I heard was bird skins being dropped into bin liners." She rustled the bag. "When she's nearly done, she sends the raven back down to the Darwin exhibit. The bird picks up the stone in its beak, flies up and throws it down onto the case, smashing the glass and setting off the alarm. Bus Stop Girl knows that everyone will rush to the Darwin exhibit. She finishes gathering the birds on her list, putting them into a second bag. That's what I heard." Ava held up the other bag. "She sneaks to the lift, takes it down to the lower ground floor, runs to the bathroom with the broken window, throws the bags through and climbs out. The raven is waiting outside for her and can warn her if anyone is coming. They sprint across the grass to the woods. The raven stands watch while she runs to the hole that was dug before the robbery..."

"I knew that was a clue," Terry said.

"She drops the two bags inside and covers it up with twigs and ivy. Then she goes along the same path we did, round to the playground. She sits in the bus stop watching the police, waiting for a bus."

There was silence.

"Bus Stop Girl didn't think anyone would notice the Wallace Room theft for a while. When she sees the extra police arriving, she realizes it's been discovered. She still has the list in her pocket. She screws it up, drops it down the back of the bench where it gets stuck to a bit of bubblegum!" Ava looked around the room triumphantly.

"It does explain the smashed window," Tara said, sounding doubtful.

"And the high crack on the case for Darwin's finches," Terry said, sounding disbelieving.

"And how the thief got into the Wallace Room," Jack admitted, "but…"

"Sherlock Holmes says" – Ava lifted a finger – "'when you have eliminated the impossible, whatever remains, however improbable, must be the truth.'"

"Your entire theory is based on the assumption that the raven is working with the girl and that no grown-ups are involved?" Twitch asked.

"Yes," Ava replied. "But for it to stand up, we need to find out if there are any girls out there who train ravens."

"But, *why* did she do it?" Jack frowned as he puzzled through Ava's theory. "What is her motive? It doesn't fit with the fashion designer suspect profile or the taxidermist."

"I don't know," Ava admitted. "But I think I'm on to something. It's the only theory that makes sense of all the clues. And I know for a fact that old Stickler won't figure it out in a million years; a kid pulling off a museum heist? He'd never believe it was possible."

OZURU UNDERCOVER

When Ozuru knocked on Tara's front door the next morning, the girls were waiting.

"Morning!" Dr Sawa greeted them, as they clambered into his car. "I'm delighted you've given me an excuse to go to the fly-tying conference. It's something I've wanted to do for years." He started the engine. "Buckle up; we've got a bit of a drive ahead of us."

Ava's phone buzzed in her pocket. It was a message from Tippi. Today was the last day of Tippi's school trip. She tapped a reply.

Hi Tip, I'm in Briddvale with Tara. We're investigating the Swan Museum Heist. I was there when it happened! Hope your trip was fun? A Xxx

"I can't believe I haven't seen Tippi for a whole week," Ava said, slipping her phone back into her pocket.

"Do you miss her?" Tara asked.

"I didn't think I would," Ava admitted. "But, yeah, I have."

Her phone buzzed, then buzzed again and again, vibrating like an insistent bumblebee.

What!!!

NO!!!

Don't solve it yet.

Not without me.

I'm on the coach home.

I can't believe you're solving a mystery without me!

I'll come as early as I can tomorrow.

What are you doing now?

Are all the Twitchers there?

Do they miss me?

I need to know EVERYTHING!!!!

Ava chuckled as she replied.

On my way to do some undercover investigating with Tara and Ozuru. Will tell you everything when you get here. Can't talk now. A xx

"There's a chance Tippi may turn up at six o'clock tomorrow morning," Ava said to Tara, turning off her phone. "I told her about the case and she's desperate to be here."

As they drove through Briddvale, Ava looked out of the window at the little town with affection.

She was confident she was right about the girl and the raven but knew she didn't have enough pieces of the puzzle to convince the others. She didn't want to upset Ozuru, but she didn't think the fishing conference would turn up any leads. Jack and Pam were spending the morning searching online for people who sold feathers to fashion designers and looking into gangs who stole antiquities. Secretly, Ava wished she was with them.

Ozuru turned around in the front seat. "Have you got your backstory prepared?"

"No," Tara admitted and Ava shook her head. "Do you have one?"

"Of course – you've got to have a backstory if you're going undercover. I brought this." He held up a book called *The Salmon Fly* by George M. Kelson. "This is the fly-tiers' Bible. I'm going to tell people that I'm learning to tie my first Victorian salmon fly and I want the real feathers to do it properly."

"Oooh, that's good." Tara looked at Ava. "What should our stories be?"

"We shouldn't pretend to know about fishing," Ava said. "That could go wrong very quickly."

"What if we're there with our parents and bored because we don't like fishing, but when we see feathers we get excited because we make hats?"

"Hats?" Ava lifted an eyebrow. "What kind of hats? Top hats?"

Ozuru laughed.

"All right, you think of a cover story that involves us wanting to buy feathers," Tara said, crossing her arms.

"I'm more likely to make feather earrings than hats," Ava said.

"Earrings? Oh yes." Tara let her arms drop. "That's much more believable."

"Dr Sawa" – Ava leaned forward – "where do people who tie flies get their feathers from?"

"Some feathers are synthetic and made from nylon, some are dyed chicken feathers. These are easy to come by. The most expensive feathers come from real birds. The rarest come from old birds but they're hard to get hold of. There are strict laws about the trading of parts of endangered creatures."

"Where do people get old birds' feathers?" Tara asked.

"Feather merchants scour antique shops and house-clearance sales for taxidermy dioramas, or vintage clothes, or hats with feathers."

As she watched the countryside zip by her window, Ava thought how odd it was that fishermen would seek out old ladies' hats to pluck the feathers and catch fish. All that money and effort to create something that could only be used once.

The car slowed as they entered another town and Ozuru pointed to a flat concrete building up ahead. "That's it."

Dr Sawa parked in the community centre car park, and they got out. Staring at the squat rectangular building, Ava felt a flicker of curiosity about what she might find inside.

"Let's investigate!" Ozuru said, charging towards the entrance.

Through the doors, two women were sitting chatting behind a table. Dr Sawa greeted them and paid the entrance fee. One woman took the money; the other gave them each a ticket.

Beyond a set of double doors was an echoing hall that reminded Ava of the gym where she did her free-running class. Four aisles of tables ran the length of the room. Behind each table were people selling fishing wares. The place was thronging with happy anglers, carrying totes stuffed with their purchases. The air reverberated with pleasant chatter and the squeak of rubber-soled shoes on the sprung wooden floor.

"I'm going to take a look at the fishing rods," Dr Sawa said, rubbing his hands together. "Come and find me when you're done detecting."

"Dad!" Ozuru protested, glancing over his shoulders. "Shhhh! You'll give us away."

"Oops. Sorry." Dr Sawa chuckled to himself as he disappeared into the crowd.

"Should we split up?" Tara asked.

"What if someone discovers something?" Ozuru said.

"Each stall has a flag with a number." Ava pointed to the nearest stand selling bait, alive and wriggling. A long, thin rod was strapped to the table leg and at the top, above head height, was a white rectangle of laminated card saying A12. "If we see something suspicious, we'll send a message to the others with the stall number closest to our location. If you receive a message, go straight to that stall." She took out her phone and turned it on.

"Good idea," Tara said.

"OK." Ozuru surveyed the room, clutching his fly-tying book to his chest. "I'll go this way."

Taking the middle aisle, Ava sauntered past stalls with galoshes and hats, books and baits, nets and hooks. She observed everything keenly, but soon realized she didn't know what fly-tying looked like.

Her heart jumped as she felt her phone buzz. She yanked it out.

What's happening now? Are you wearing a disguise? Is it exciting? I wish I was there.

Ava shoved her phone back into her pocket, irked by Tippi's message. The fishing conference was not exciting. Her phone buzzed again. Why wouldn't her sister leave her alone?

P27

It was from Ozuru!

Ava looked up at the flag closest to her. D13. Weaving through the shoal of avid anglers, she headed for Ozuru's aisle. She spotted him standing in a huddle of people, watching an elderly man with hair like thistledown. His face was weatherworn and threaded with tiny purple veins. On the table in front of him, Ava saw reels of coloured thread, copper wire, a bag of tiny beads, pliers, scissors, superglue and an assortment of feathers, all laid out neatly on a craft mat. Held at eye height by a clamp was a gold hook. The man was staring fixedly through thick-lensed glasses at it, as he skilfully wrapped thread round the hook. Ava edged through the huddle, watching as the man picked up a feather, snipped off a two-centimetre section and used a black thread to attach it to the hook, winding it over the feather so that tufts stuck out.

She came to stand beside Ozuru, who elbowed her to make her look down. He was using sign language. She missed the first part of the message.

"Feathers?" she signed, pointing her finger at the table.

Ozuru gave the tiniest shake of his head. *"Look left."*

Intrigued by Ozuru's secrecy, Ava moved just her eyes, and saw Tara at the next stand pretending to be interested in fishing lures. Ava shot Ozuru a puzzled look.

"Two men. Suspicious," he signed.

Then she saw them. Behind Tara, two men in their early to mid-twenties were talking to the stall owner. One of the men was beefy. A baseball cap hid the top of his face. He had a bomber jacket slung over his shoulder. His biceps bulged out of the arms of his T-shirt and his jeans were stretched tight around his muscly legs. The second man was tall and slender with an arrogant manner. His blond hair was swept to one side. He wore a crisp white shirt, open at the neck, and his navy chinos had a sharp crease. The pair looked out of place amongst the comfortably dressed fishing fans.

Ozuru nudged Ava, then signed, *"They asked him"* – he pointed at the elderly fly-tier – *"if he wanted to buy rare feathers."*

The men were feather dealers! Ava watched the men and suddenly her theory about the girl in the bus stop didn't seem like such a good one. If they were here to sell feathers, maybe Stickler was right: perhaps a gang was behind the robbery.

Acting as if her phone were ringing, Ava stepped backwards out of the huddle. She glanced at the screen, as if to see who was calling, opening her camera with a tap of her thumb. Holding the phone to her ear, she turned so it faced the two men and, quickly as she could, Ava hammered her finger against the screen, taking a series of photos. Then she moved back to stand beside Ozuru.

"I got pictures," she whispered.

Ozuru gave a nod of approval, then signed, *"Follow them. I'll stay here to talk to the man."* He pointed to the fly-tier.

Ava waved to Tara, as if just spotting her, and went over to the rainbow display of brightly coloured, minnow-sized plastic fishes. But the suspicious men had finished their business with the stall owner and were moving away through the crowd.

"Those men," Tara whispered. "They were asking if

the stall owner wanted to buy real vintage feathers, or if he knew anyone who might be interested!"

"So that's what feather dealers look like," Ava said, watching the men stride away.

"What do we do?" Tara's voice was high with excitement.

"Follow them." Ava moved after them.

Tara grabbed Ava's hand as they hurried through the crowd, their eyes locked on the backs of the two men who were heading for the exit. The burly guy paused to put on his bomber jacket while the taller one took out keys with a chunky black fob.

"They're going to the car park," Ava whispered. "Quick, this way." She ducked round two tables to a fire door propped open by a brick. The two girls hurried out of the building and sprinted along the path to the car park.

Scurrying behind a line of parked cars, the girls watched the two men cross the car park. The blond man held out his keys. The lights of a black sports car flashed.

"That's their car," Ava whispered. "We need to get a picture of the number plate."

She dropped down, moving closer, hiding behind a laurel bush a few metres from the supercar. Tara crouched beside her with her phone out. Peeping over the bush, Tara held up her phone, zoomed in, took the picture and dropped back down. "JA55 PER," she read from the screen of her phone.

Peering through the laurel leaves, Ava watched the blond man open the car door, glance at his watch, then slide into the driver's seat. He pulled his ringing phone from his pocket.

"What? Yes. It's a bunch of weird people who smell of fish. How the hell would I know if they've got money? They don't dress like they do. Right. Yup. Will do." He hung up, tossing his phone into the cup holder in front of the gear stick and saying, "Idiotic old man."

"Who is?" asked the beefy bloke, taking off his baseball cap to reveal a shaved head. He folded himself into the passenger seat.

"Who d'you think? Dad. Don't you think it's about time he retired?"

"He'll never retire."

"I'm sick of these crackpot schemes," the blond one grumbled. "We should be in the big league."

"Are you talking about football?"

"Yes. I'm talking about football." Sarcasm dripped from every word, but the beefy bloke didn't notice. With an expression of disdain, the blond man shut the door, pulled on his seatbelt, revved the engine and reversed.

Ava watched the car leave, while Tara wrote down what the men had said in her casebook.

Flashing their tickets at the ladies on the door as they went back inside, the girls headed for the stand where they'd left Ozuru watching the elderly fly-tier. As they approached, Ava saw that the demonstration was over and Ozuru was behind the table talking to the elderly man. He had his book open and was pointing at a picture. Ava put her hand on Tara's arm and they hung back.

"I want to make a Durham Ranger," Ozuru was saying.

"That's a bold choice for a novice!" The man hooted.

"Do you think it's too hard?"

The man looked over his glasses and smiled at Ozuru. "Practice and a steady hand are all it takes."

"I hope to get as good as you one day," Ozuru said. "What feathers do you use?"

"Chicken feathers," the fly-tier replied.

"Oh! Don't you use the ones in the recipes?" Ozuru pointed to his book again. "The real ones."

"You mustn't know much about birds if you think those feathers are easy to come by." He chuckled.

"But you can get them?" Ozuru asked.

"Only if you're prepared to part with a hundred pounds a feather," the old man said, "which I am not."

"A hundred pounds!" Ozuru looked genuinely shocked.

"You don't need to go spending a heap of money on feathers, son." The man tutted, shaking his head. "You need experience."

"Where do you buy them from?"

"I told you. I don't. There's some silly folk who go in for that kind of thing in the fly-tiers club, but not me."

"A club? That sounds fun. I'd love to meet other fly-tiers."

"Well, here." The man took a scrap of paper from the table and scribbled something down on it, handing it to Ozuru. "But don't go wasting all your pocket money on one feather. Chicken feathers will do just fine."

"I won't. Thank you for talking to me, sir."

"Malcolm Wallis."

"Thank you, Mr Wallis."

Ozuru came hurrying over to Ava and Tara, his dark eyes shining. "Did you follow the two men?" he asked.

"Let's go sit down." Ava nodded, pointing to the corner of the hall.

"I think I've worked out the blond man's name," Tara said as they sat on the floor, clustered tightly together.

"What! How?" Ava asked.

"He had the keys and drove, so I'm guessing the black car was his." She held up her phone and Ava saw the photograph of it. "Take a look at his licence plate. It's personalized."

"JA55 PER." Ozuru spelled it out.

"If we take the 55 to be an S," Tara said. "J-A-S-P-E-R. Jasper."

"Oh!" Ava was impressed. "I think you're right!"

"Good deduction," Ozuru said.

"You're the one who spotted they were feather dealers," Tara replied, looking bashful.

"They were talking to Mr Wallis, before he started his fly-tying demonstration," Ozuru said. "The blond man, Jasper, was showing him photographs. I couldn't see what of, but I think it was bird skins. Mr Wallis was shaking his head. I heard him say, "I'm a bit past robbing banks, and I'd have to, to afford one of those." Ozuru looked thrilled. "I think those men might be the ones who robbed the Swan Museum."

"Yes," Tara agreed. "When I was pretending to look at the little plastic fish—"

"Lures," Ozuru corrected her.

"Yes. Lures. Well, I heard bits of what Jasper was saying to the stall owner. He said he'd got his hands on an auction lot of rare Victorian birds and was looking to sell the feathers. The stall holder seemed interested, and they exchanged details."

It stung Ava that her Bus Stop Girl theory had been so easily dismissed, but she had to admit the two shady men seemed more likely to be criminals. "It was a great idea to come here, Ozuru," she admitted, and he flushed with pleasure. "I think you've got us our first concrete lead."

15
RAVEN GIRL

Ava, Tara and Ozuru ate their sandwiches in the car on the way back to Briddvale, and Dr Sawa dropped them off in the Aves Wood car park. The three Twitchers hurried along the main footpath, eager to reach the others and tell them what they'd discovered. At the hide, Twitch and Jack were standing outside chatting.

"I was just telling Twitch," Jack said, hailing them, "Pam and I didn't get very far with our search for black market feather merchants. Most designers go out of their way to tell you they use legally farmed ostrich feathers."

"Terry's on his way," Twitch told Ozuru as they went into the cabin.

"Speaking of Terry," Tara said, sitting on her tree stump. "Does anyone know what Pam's blackmail video is about?"

"I asked him," Ozuru said, "but Terry's so cross with

146

me for thinking he and Pam were dating, he won't say."

"I'm dying to know." Tara giggled. "It must be really embarrassing."

"How was the fishing thing?" Jack asked Ava.

"Well, it looks like my theory about Bus Stop Girl and her pet raven is wrong." Ava nudged Ozuru. "Go on, tell them."

Ozuru took his seat at the table and recounted his spotting of the two suspicious men trying to sell feathers.

"I got photos of them." Ava held up her phone for them to see.

"And I got their number plate." Tara held up hers. "We worked out that the blond man is called Jasper."

"Well done." Jack was impressed.

"This is brilliant!" Twitch agreed.

"I'll tell you who's not brilliant," Terry said, as he came through the doorway. "Pam. I bumped into her on my way here. She's looking for us. Says she's got a lead. She refused to tell me what it was because I wouldn't bring her to the hide. She's waiting on Crowther Bridge."

"We've got a lead too," Ozuru told him. "I saw two men asking people if they wanted to buy vintage feathers at the fishing conference. We think they might be the thieves."

"I wonder if they were trying to set up a fence," Jack said, thinking out loud. "Someone to sell the feathers for them, for a cut of the profit."

"I've got information about a fly-tiers club," Ozuru said. "When I get home, I'm going to register on their website and ask if anyone knows about new feathers being made available. I might end up talking to whoever has the birds."

"That's the kind of detecting that leads to an arrest," Jack said enthusiastically.

"Nice one." Terry grinned at Ozuru.

"The sooner we can find them, the better," Twitch said. "We need to get the birds back *before* they're taken apart to be sold. Those two men drumming up interest in the bird skin feathers is bad news."

"That's not easy," Jack admitted.

"Although," Terry said, "if you were a criminal ... you wouldn't immediately go online and start selling rare bird-of-paradise feathers the day after you stole them. It would create a trail straight back to you. It would make much more sense to use a fence, like Jack said, and that would take time to set up. If they're smart, the thieves will wait until the heat dies down a bit."

"We shouldn't keep Pam waiting," Tara reminded them.

"I wonder what her lead is." Jack got up. "She didn't have one when I left her house."

"She seemed pretty excited," Terry said.

Leaving the hide, Ava broke into a run, speeding through the trees, enjoying the power of her body as she leaped over thorny tangles of scrub and knobbly roots, following the river. She spotted Pam sitting on the bridge in her pink puffer coat, with her legs dangling through the railings. Glancing over her shoulder, Ava paused so the others could catch up.

"Don't know why you made me wait here," Pam said to Terry as they all trooped onto the bridge. "If I wanted to find your secret hideout, I could, you know." She swept her hair over her shoulder. "It's probably a hovel made of mud and sticks."

"Did you bring us here to insult us?" Terry asked cheerfully.

"No." Pam looked at Ava. "After Jack left, I thought I'd have a search to see if I could find anything on your Bus Stop Girl." She handed her a piece of paper. "Take a look at this."

Ava stared at the newspaper article. It was from two years ago. It had a black-and-white photo of a fresh-faced girl with a gap-toothed smile, her dark hair pulled into a ponytail.

"Well?" Pam asked eagerly. "Is it her?"

"Is it who?" Jack came to Ava's side.

"Yes. It's the girl from the bus stop," Ava croaked and, to her surprise, she felt like crying. The difference between the happy girl in the picture and the hunched, bruised girl in the bus stop was shocking.

Clearing her throat, Ava swallowed, giving herself a moment to recover. "Her name is Rae Rackem," she said, skimming the article. "It says her parents died in a fire."

"Look at the headline," Pam said. "'Girl Rae Rescued by Raven'. That's how I found the article."

"The girl is bonded to a raven?" Twitch's voice was tinged with awe as he leaned in to see. They were all crowded around Ava now.

Ava read the article slowly to make sure she understood every word.

A fire had burned down Rae Rackem's home. It had started in the middle of the night, in the kitchen. Someone had left the gas on. There had been an explosion. Rae's parents had been asleep in their beds. The smoke had suffocated them before the flames got to them.

Rae had been nursing an abandoned raven chick back to health in the shed. She had wanted to camp out with the bird, but her parents had forbidden it. That night, after they'd gone to bed, Rae had crept out of the house with a roll mat and sleeping bag and gone to sleep in the shed with the young bird. The explosion had woken her up. The fire brigade had found Rae in the neighbours' garden, in her nightie, clutching a cardboard box with the raven in it, frightened half to death.

Ava was stunned. The black feather in the Wallace Room belonged to a raven. This raven was bonded to the Bus Stop Girl. Had she had been right after all? But what had happened to little Rae Rackem to turn her into a museum robber?

Ava handed the article to Jack and Terry, feeling hollow. Tippi was almost the same age Rae had been when the fire had happened. She was always rescuing injured creatures too. Ava suddenly missed her little sister so much her stomach ached.

"We need to find her," Ava said with grim determination. "I think Rae Rackem is in terrible trouble."

16

FROM THE ASHES

Ava's mum arrived with Tippi the next morning, just after breakfast. Ava swept her little sister up into a bear hug. She hadn't been able to get Rae Rackem out of her head since reading Pam's article.

"Ow! You're crushing me!" Tippi protested as she struggled out of Ava's arms.

Ava didn't even mind when her mum scolded her, saying she'd not forgotten or forgiven her for running away from the school coach, and that she'd have to deal with the consequences of her actions when she got home.

Ava's mum stayed for a cup of tea with the Dabiris, then kissed her girls goodbye, eliciting promises of good and helpful behaviour.

"I brought your clothes," Tippi said, dumping Ava's gym bag onto Tara's bedroom floor.

Ava pounced on it. "Are my trackies in here?"

"She's been wearing the same socks since Friday," Tara told Tippi.

"Your feet are tiny," Ava grumbled. "I'm a size seven. Anyway, I washed them in the sink last night. They're clean."

"I'm a size three," Tara told Tippi.

"Snap! Same as me."

Taking out her favourite black tracksuit, a pair of sports socks and her running shoes, Ava grabbed her sister with her free arm and hugged her again. "Thanks. Right, I'm off to the bathroom to get changed."

As she left the room, Ava heard Tippi saying, "Why's Ava being weird?"

Dressed in her own clothes, Ava felt much more herself and ready for anything. When she returned to the bedroom, Tippi was sitting on the bed cross-legged, eyes wide, mouth open, listening as Tara told her everything that had happened since Ava had arrived in Briddvale.

"That poor raven girl." Tippi looked at Ava. "Do you think she's all right?"

"We're going to try and find her today," Ava assured her.

"The newspaper article named the road her house

was on," Tara said. "It's called Cygnet Close. It's in Swanhurst, the same town as the museum."

"We're going to visit it today and search for clues," Ava told her. "Hey, did Mum give you any money?"

"Ka-ching!" Tippi pulled a bundle of notes from her pocket. "She says we have to buy Tara lunch and get chocolates for the Dabiris before we go home."

"Excellent," Ava said, swiping the cash and jamming it into her pocket.

"Hey!" Tippi started to complain.

"If you're coming with us," Ava said, "you've got to get ready. We're meeting the others at the station in thirty minutes. Dress warm – we're going to be outdoors."

Tippi didn't need telling twice. She pulled her sling bag over her head, checking she had her travel binoculars, a notebook and pen.

When the three girls arrived at the station, the chilly air was thick with winter mist. It was too cold to sit on the bench, so they huddled together on the platform. The boys arrived and immediately made a fuss of Tippi.

"I joined that fly-tying club last night," Ozuru told Ava and Tara, as Terry jigged on the spot next to him to keep warm. "There's no one posting about birds-of-paradise feathers on the forum yet. But I'm watching."

"If Jasper and that other man have got something to do with the robbery, and Rae does too, then I'm wondering what the connection is between them," Ava said.

"I've been thinking about that too." Tara nodded.

When they arrived in Swanhurst, Ozuru used his phone to direct them to Cygnet Close. It was further away from the station than the museum and in a different direction. They walked along a leafy road that ran alongside a river, then crossed it, walking past a parade of shops and out into rows of newly built terraced houses.

"My feet hurt," Tippi grumbled. "Are we nearly there?"

"Ten minutes," Ozuru replied.

When they found Cygnet Close, it was immediately clear which house had belonged to Rae Rackem. Despite two years having passed since the fire, the building was still charred and derelict. The middle of the roof was bare of tiles. Crumbling charcoal beams stuck out like the ribs of a wrecked ship. The door and windows were boarded up. There was a sign – a yellow triangle containing an exclamation mark – on the front door. Underneath it were the words: *DANGER UNSAFE BUILDING*. Beside it was a blue sign with a white exclamation mark and the words: *KEEP OUT*.

The Twitchers stood, staring at the devastated house.

"Why haven't they fixed it?" Tippi asked, sounding distressed.

"I don't know." Ava put a reassuring hand on her sister's shoulder.

"The house must belong to Rae now," Jack said.

"Let's get to work," Tara said. "Ozuru and I will speak to the neighbours on this side of the house." She pointed. "Jack, Terry, you do the other side."

"What about us?" Tippi asked Ava.

"We're going to explore the garden," Ava said.

"I want to take a look in that shed where Rae kept the raven," Twitch said.

"Me too," Ava agreed.

Double-checking the coast was clear, Twitch, Tippi and Ava snuck up the path into the overgrown front garden, cautiously approaching the scorched house. There was a side gate in a panelled fence. Ava tried the handle. It was locked. She cracked her knuckles, took four strides backwards and ran at the gate. Driving her feet into the paved path, she jumped, throwing her arms up, briefly gripping the top of the fence as she tucked her knees and propelled herself over, landing in a crouch on the other side.

Pausing, Ava listened for any outcry. She heard grumbling traffic, a bossy robin, and a passing plane. She stood up and unbolted the gate. Tippi and Twitch slipped through.

"You know," Twitch whispered, "you'd make an excellent cat burglar."

Ava grinned. She'd been doing free running ever since her mum had been falsely arrested. When she was angry, it was the only thing that calmed her down. After she'd discovered she was good at it, she'd taken gymnastics lessons and rock climbing to make her even better. If she had to, she was confident she could escape anyone who tried to chase her.

The back of Rae's house looked worse than the front. All that was left of the kitchen was a pile of rubble. The flat roof was slumped like melted ice cream over blackened bricks.

Ava felt Tippi's hand slip into hers.

Turning away from the house, Ava studied the garden. The lawn was a wild meadow of dead grasses, flattened and blackened by winter frost. Unruly shrubs and bushes were happily spreading, unchecked, in all directions. Birds were wintering here, and insects were feeding on the ivy flowers.

"Rae's shed." Twitch pointed to a potting shed

beneath a big silver birch. It was cloaked in ivy. The door was half hidden by an exuberant holly bush heavy with blood-red berries.

"Do we go in?" asked Tippi.

It felt like an invasion of privacy, but they had to find Rae Rackem to be able to help her. The shed was the only place which might hold a clue to her whereabouts. Ava peered through the little window. It was dark inside. She tried the handle. "It's locked."

"Look." Tippi was crouching beside the holly tree trunk. Between her feet was a cheerful garden gnome. It looked like it had been painted by a child. Tippi had tilted it backwards. Under its feet was a key.

"How did you know that was there?" Twitch marvelled.

"I thought about where I would hide a key," Tippi admitted, "and there it was."

Ava took the key and unlocked the door. She expected the shed to be full of cobwebs and dust, but to her surprise it was clean inside. On the floor was a roll mat – like the kind you slept on when camping – two sofa cushions and a rolled-up sleeping bag, neatly piled together.

"She still comes here!" Ava said to Twitch, who was standing in the doorway.

Tippi squatted down by a carrier bag in the furthest corner of the shed and peered inside, pulling out a bottle of water, a half-eaten chocolate bar, a pen and a notebook. She let out a little gasp. "It says 'Escape Plan' on the cover."

"Put it back." Ava felt a pang of guilt. "We shouldn't be touching her things."

"I was investigating." Tippi put the bag down and retreated. "I wasn't going to take anything."

"Ava, Tippi," Twitch said in a low voice. "There's a raven overhead."

Ava's pulse quickened as Twitch backed away from the shed, keeping the bird in view. As she emerged, she heard the corvid shriek a warning *caw! caw!*

There was a scuffling noise and Ava turned her head to see the top half of a bruised face peering over the fence. Ava's eyes met Rae's. They locked for a split second then Rae disappeared. Ava heard her running away.

"I'm going after her," she told Tippi and Twitch as she ran at the fence, vaulting over.

17

FREE RUNNING

Ava landed with a thud in an alleyway. It took her a second to get her bearings. She jogged after Rae. The ground was slippery. The skeletal corpses of leaves had been pulped by human feet and hardened by winter frosts.

The rhythmic thud of Ava's footsteps accompanied her thoughts as her white breath become one with the winter mist. Had Rae recognized Ava from the bus stop? She didn't want to frighten the girl; she wanted to help. Ava could catch up with her easily, but chasing someone wasn't a friendly thing to do. What if she caught up with the girl and Rae refused to talk to her? What if she didn't want Ava's help? But Rae had a notebook labelled *Escape Plan*. You didn't need an escape plan if your life was happy. What if Rae was running towards the place the stolen birds were hidden? Ava put on a burst of speed.

The alley came to an end and she found herself near a parade of shops they'd passed on their way to Cygnet Close. Her heart was beating loudly as she surveyed the street. Rae was nowhere to be seen. Ava had assumed she'd be able to spot her when she came out of the alley. The girl could only have been a hundred or so metres ahead of her. She had to be here somewhere. Perhaps she was hiding.

Ava heard a far-off shout and looked up the road to see the Twitchers running out of Cygnet Close. Jack was in the lead with Twitch hard on his heels. Behind them, Tara was running, holding Tippi's hand. Tippi's legs were shorter than everyone else's; she had to take more strides to keep up.

Twitch pointed to the sky. Ava looked up to see a raven circling above the fried chicken restaurant. She glimpsed Rae's head, peeping round a brick chimney pot. She was on the roof! How had she got up there?

Ava's brain switched into free-running mode. She scanned the building for grips, shelves, railings and ledges as she took her fingerless climbing gloves from her coat pocket and put them on. She sprinted to the newsagent on the end of the row of shops, running three paces up the wall and hurling her hands up to grab the edge of the flat roof of the lean-to. Taking advantage of her upward momentum, Ava locked her arms and swung her legs sideways, as if using the vaulting horse in gym class. When her feet were at a ninety-degree angle, she relaxed her arms and lurched forward, rolling onto the roof, before immediately springing to her feet.

Above her, the raven was making a short, shrill rasping noise over and over again. Ava ignored the bird as she searched for a way up. There was an iron girder sticking out of the wall about a metre from the apex of the triangular roof. It looked like it had once been part of a big winch. Below it was a window, and beside that, a cast iron drainpipe.

Speed was of the essence.

Gravity was the enemy.

Running the two steps to the wall, Ava leaped onto the window ledge with the grace of a mountain goat, leaning out to grab and scramble up the drainpipe, keeping her eyes locked on the iron girder. Throwing out a hand, Ava gripped it, letting her body swing so she could get her second hand on the girder. Pulling herself up, she twisted to sit on it.

"Look up, not down," she whispered to herself. "Focus."

Drawing her feet up, Ava positioned them carefully on the girder, then, with arms outstretched, she slowly stood up as if she were on a balance beam.

In her peripheral vision she thought she saw the dark shapes of the Twitchers gathering below. She didn't allow herself to look. One gust of wind would send her tumbling to the concrete, but thankfully the icy air was still.

She lifted her arms and felt along the tiles of the roof. Her fingers found two metal brackets. Gripping them tightly, Ava pushed down into the beam with her feet and bounced up, pulling her body higher, praying the brackets would hold as she leaned her weight forward so that her stomach lay on the roof tiles. Running her feet up the wall, using the friction to give her forward momentum, she lurched and rolled her body, until she was lying on her back on the sloped roof.

Ava's breath was coming in gasps as she stared up at the powder-pewter sky. Her heart was drumming against her ribs. She felt the delayed rush of fear as she allowed herself to acknowledge the danger of her climb and how much her arms ached. But she'd done it! She was on the roof!

Coming onto her stomach, Ava pulled herself onto her knees. Her whole body was trembling. She waited for the shaking to pass, trying to breathe calmly, eventually raising her head so that the Twitchers could see her. She gave them a thumbs up.

Hearing a scraping sound, Ava turned. Rae was sitting astride the roof apex several shops along, hurriedly shuffling away.

How had she got up here? Surely not the way Ava had?

Two shops along, Ava spotted a ladder bolted to the side of the building. It climbed right up onto the roof. "That would've been a safer way to do it," she muttered to herself.

Checking her muscles with each movement, Ava carefully crawled up the roof, wary of loose tiles.

Once she too was sitting, straddling the apex, she paused. The tiles curving over the peak reminded her of a balance beam. She was really good on the beam. But if she raced after Rae, the girl might panic and fall. Ava didn't want that. So, Ava waited and watched, gathering her strength and recovering her breath.

At the end of the parade of shops was a narrow gap followed by a low block of flats with a level roof. Ava waited until Rae had safely clambered and jumped onto it.

Placing her gloved hands on the tiled beam in front of her, Ava lifted her bottom a couple of inches, swinging her legs forward and back, before pushing down with her hands and bringing her feet onto the curved tiles.

With her arms out for balance, Ava stood up, then ran, lightly, as fast as she dared, speeding along the apex of the roof, eyes on the path ahead.

When she reached the end, Ava leaped, tucking her head and throwing her legs over, somersaulting as she would in her beam dismount. She landed with a slight bend in her knees to absorb the impact, her arms above her head.

Rae was three flat rooftops away, staring at Ava with a look of shock on her face.

"I just want to talk to you," Ava called out. "I'm on your side."

But Rae turned and fled.

Ava sighed. This wasn't going the way she wanted. She needed to try not to frighten Rae, but how? Keeping her eyes on the route Rae was taking across the buildings' rooftops and balconies, Ava followed slowly so as not to scare the girl into making a false move.

As she gradually gained on her, Ava risked glancing down into the street. She couldn't see the Twitchers any more. She was on her own.

Clambering into a decked garden with raised flower beds, Ava sprinted across it. There was only one rooftop between her and Rae now. The raven was flying above the girl's head, watching her.

"Please!" Ava called out. "Rae! I just want to talk to you."

Rae froze at the sound of her name and turned her head.

"What do you want?" Rae shouted. "Why were you in my shed?"

"I'm sorry," Ava called back. "I shouldn't have gone in there. I didn't realize... I was looking for you." She took a few steps nearer.

"Why?"

"Because ... I want to help you." She moved a little closer.

To Ava's surprise Rae laughed. It was a hollow, haunting sound. "You can't help me," she said bitterly. "No one can."

The raven dropped down, landing on Rae's shoulder. It croaked at Ava, as if echoing what Rae had said.

"No one except you, Caliban," Rae said to the bird, leaning her head towards the raven. The bird rubbed its beak against her cheek.

"Caliban!" the raven squawked.

Ava blinked, unsure if she'd heard the bird speak or imagined it.

"Leave us alone," Rae called out, turning away.

"But..." Ava didn't know what the right thing to say

was. "I know about the theft at the museum and" – she moved forwards – "if we went to the police together…"

"If you want to help me," Rae replied angrily, "you'll swear right now that you'll never talk to the police about me, or what happened at the museum, *ever*!"

"But…" Ava took another step forward.

Rae's expression clouded over. "You're just like the rest of them," she shouted. "Caliban." She pointed at Ava. "Attack!"

18

UNDERNEATH
THE ARCHES

Like darkness falling, the raven descended. It gave a strangled croak. Ava cried out, throwing her arms up to protect her face. She heard the terrifying *clack* of the bird's beak and felt a dart of pain at the top of her right ear.

"*Ow!*" Ava tried to look up, but the bird was behind her now. She felt a sharp blow to the back of her head, as if a stone had been thrown at her. A tide of panic surged through Ava's chest. She needed to get off the roof. The raven was dangerous. She was suddenly disorientated. Sharp claws gripped her shoulder as a beakful of hair was torn from her scalp.

"Enough!" Ava snapped angrily, throwing herself forward into a roly-poly and springing to her feet again.

Caliban flapped his wings, rising to get out of her path.

For a second, Ava was free. She glanced around. There was no sign of Rae. The next-door roof had a fire escape ladder reaching down the back of the building. Before Caliban could dive at her again, Ava was running. With a leap and a roll, she was on the next roof, sprinting to the ladder. She grabbed the sides and had placed her foot on a rung when she heard a deep, gurgling *caw*. A black missile hurtled towards her head. Gripping the ladder tightly, Ava tucked her chin into her neck to protect her face, stifling a scream as claws scratched her scalp. Battered by the sound and sensation of flapping wings, she was knocked off balance and felt an icy jet of fear.

She closed her eyes, gripping the ladder. She must concentrate on moving one foot down a rung, then the next. How high was she? Three storeys? Four? She'd been so intent on catching up with Rae, she wasn't sure.

Her right hand blazed with pain. She instinctively let go of the ladder. Her eyes snapped open as she swung out. The knuckles of her right hand were covered in blood where Caliban had scratched her. Leaning into the ladder, Ava clamped her right hand back around the side and descended two rungs.

Caliban darted at her again, this time going for her left hand.

"Oh no you don't," Ava growled through gritted teeth.

Gripping the sides of the ladder tightly, Ava jumped her feet out so that they were on the outside of the ladder too, pressing against it. She loosened her hold and slid down like a fireman.

Ava's gloves protected her palms but not her fingertips. She cried out as they were burned by friction, but she didn't let go.

Slamming into the ground, Ava fell backwards, curling into a protective ball, holding her flayed fingers to her chest. Any second now there'd be another aerial assault from the protective raven, but, as the moments passed, none came. Eventually Ava moved her head enough to peep up at the sky.

Caliban was gone.

Ava squeezed her eyes shut as a tear rolled down her cheek. She had really mucked that up. Why had she brought up the robbery? She had scared Rae off and possibly lost her for ever.

She heard the thud of running feet.

"Ava? Oh no! *Ava!*"

Opening her eyes, Ava found she was looking up at the concerned face of Jack.

"Ava, are you OK?" He dropped to his knees beside her. "Do you need an ambulance? Did you fall?"

"I'm all right." Ava sat up so that Jack could see she didn't have any broken bones.

"The way you climbed up there, walking along the top of the roof!" Jack was shaking his head in disbelief. "I nearly had a heart attack watching you. I tried to keep up, but I lost sight of you and … and…" He stopped, looking suddenly serious. "Don't you ever do anything like that ever again, Ava."

"You sound like my mum," Ava said, giving him a wry smile.

"I mean it. That was way too dangerous."

"I didn't know you cared," Ava said glibly, batting away his concern.

Jack looked at her, his green eyes unblinking. "I do."

"I'm fine. Really. I am." Ava felt herself blushing. "I didn't fall. Rae ordered her raven to attack me. I had to slide down the ladder to escape it." She uncurled her fists and showed him the blistered skin on her fingers.

"Ava!" Jack drew in a shocked breath. "Your knuckles look bad, and what happened to your head?" He moved his hand as if to touch her cheek but then stopped himself. "It's bleeding."

"That was Caliban. He pecked and scratched me. Really. I'm OK, I'm just a bit … sore." She lifted her elbow towards him. "Help me up, would you?"

"Who's Caliban?" Jack asked, gently pulling Ava to her feet.

"Caliban is the name of Rae's raven." Ava looked past him. "Where are the others?"

"They stopped to watch you on the roof. You were moving so fast, it was all I could do to keep you in my sights!" He gave her a look of admiration and shook his head. "You're a freakin' ninja!"

Ava felt a warm glow at Jack's praise. "Yeah, but I lost Rae, didn't I?"

"*You* might've lost her," Jack said with the flash of a smile, "but I saw her come down from the rooftop. She dropped onto a balcony and ran down an internal stairway. She walked into the street right in front of me. I thought you would be following. I watched her as I waited for you. When you didn't come, I got worried and came looking."

"Did you see which way she went?" Ava asked.

"I know exactly where she's gone," Jack said.

"Then what are we doing? Let's get after her."

"Maybe we should go to the chemist and get your cuts looked at first," Jack said.

"I'm not losing her." Ava shoved her fists into her pockets, walking away from him.

"Fine." Jack sighed, pointing in the opposite direction. "But it's this way."

When they emerged on the street, there was no sign of the others. Ava looked enquiringly at Jack. He nodded to the bridge which crossed the river. They jogged over it, then Jack ducked under the railing and slipped his way down a steep path, to the riverbank. Ava followed him.

"She went in there," Jack said, as Ava came to stand beside him.

Through a curtain of ivy and brambles, Ava spied the opening of a brick tunnel, a little higher than the river.

"I think it's an overflow tunnel," Jack said.

"Where do you think it goes?" Ava ducked, peering in, but she couldn't see more than a few metres ahead.

"I guess we're going to find out," Jack said, taking a torch from his coat pocket. He pulled aside the curtain of plants. Ava went in first and he followed.

The tunnel was about a metre and a half high at its tallest point. Ava had to stoop to avoid the mildew and moss growing from the oozing walls. She couldn't see the end; it went on into darkness.

"Here," Jack said softly, and his voice echoed eerily off the walls. "Put your arm through mine. If you slip, I'll stop you from falling."

"I won't fall," Ava said, letting him wind his arm around hers.

"Probably not, but you don't want dirty water getting into the cuts on your hands," he said. "If I fall, you can let go and have a good laugh."

Ava didn't like depending on other people, but Jack had a way of making it OK. She smiled at him in the dark, knowing he couldn't see.

The only noises in the tunnel were their footsteps, occasionally the splash of a puddle, and the steady drip of moisture from the walls. As they walked, their path lit by Jack's torch, Ava wondered what was above their heads – a road, perhaps, or people's houses? The distant sounds of traffic felt a world away.

"This is a brilliant way of getting around with no one seeing you," Jack observed. "Useful if you're a criminal."

Ava shivered at the thought of encountering someone down here, and Jack hugged her arm closer. After they'd been walking for what felt like an age, she saw the glow of daylight in the distance. "We're nearly through."

A loud rumble sounded and, for a second, Ava panicked, thinking that a great flood of water was rushing down the tunnel to wash them away. She saw nothing coming and realized the *drip! drip!* inside the tunnel was close but the rumble was far away. "I think it's a train," she said.

"We must be near the station."

They walked a little faster, needing the torch less as daylight reached them. When they emerged, they were in a dried-up ditch, choked with litter and weeds. A metre and a half above the tunnel, Ava saw a deep layer of grey stones: ballast. On it were railway tracks and, in the distance, she thought she spied the train station.

"I guess the tunnel is to protect the railway from flooding," Jack said.

"Which way did Rae go?" Ava wondered.

The both realized at the same moment that they were still holding on to one another, and uncoupled.

"Rae won't have crossed the tracks," Jack said. "That's too dangerous." He scrambled over the ditch and climbed up to a place where there had once been a fence but now there was a gap, framed by nettles. "There's a lane down there."

A pinging noise made Jack take out his phone. "The others are at the train station. Shall I tell them we'll meet them there?"

Ava nodded, passing him and scrambling down the steep incline to the tarmac lane. "There are railway arches here, under the train bridge."

The first one was a mechanic's workshop. The shutter was up, and a radio was blaring out a rock song.

Ava could hear the buzz of machines and the hiss of pressurized air. A glossy metal sandwich board outside said they did MOTs without appointments. The next arch had a glass front through which she could see people on running machines and lifting weights. It was a gym. The one after that was a hairdresser.

"Oh no!" Ava froze.

Beyond the hairdresser's, parked in front of an arch with a closed blue shuttered front, was a car she recognized: a black two-seater with the number plate JA55 PER. She grabbed Jack's arm, sucking in air as pain shot up her fingers.

"What is it?" Jack looked alarmed.

"That car," Ava whispered. "It belongs to the two men we saw at the fishing conference yesterday."

They stared at the railway arch. There was a door next to the blue shuttered front. It had the number 645 painted clumsily on it in black. Bolted to the iron girder above the shutter was a battered old sign that read:

PESTOKIL
Total Wipeout
Quality Pest Control
CALL 0808 8008 8888

They shuffled closer. Jack took pictures. "It looks like there might be a connection between our raven girl and the two feather traders," he whispered.

The door beside the shutter opened and Ava yanked Jack backwards to stand beside her, pretending to look at the price list in the hairdresser's window.

"Don't know why Dad keeps her around," Ava heard a man say. She risked a sideways glance and saw the arrogant blond man from the fishing conference striding to his car. "She's more trouble than she's worth. If I were him, I'd tie her up, put her in a sack, and throw her in the river."

"She's only a kid, Jasper." It was the muscle-bound man with the shaved head. "She did the job, didn't she? Give her a break. She's our cousin, after all."

"That bird of hers gives me the creeps." Jasper pointed his keys at his car and Ava heard it unlock. "One day, when it's not looking, I'm going to wring its neck."

"Jasper…"

"If you love them so much, Phil" – Jasper slid into the driver's seat – "you can be the one to track her next time she pulls a disappearing trick."

Phil didn't reply, but opened the passenger door and got in.

"Anyway," Jasper said, "at least we know she won't be going anywhere for a few days." He laughed and then Phil laughed too.

A chill ran down Ava's spine. What did they mean?

The doors closed with a clunk and the black sports car moved soundlessly down the lane.

19
THE DEAD ZOO GANG

"Jack, we have to help Rae," Ava said as she studied the archway. Above the shutter was an iron girder and above that, a semi-circular window of toughened glass. "She could be in there. She could be hurt." She looked at the welts on her fingers. "Can you take my weight?"

"Carry you?" Jack nodded. "Of course."

"I'm thinking of something a bit more acrobatic." She pointed to the glass. "See that window? If you stand with your back against the wall, and give me a bunk up, I can step onto your shoulders and look in. I might be able to see Rae."

"Er, yeah." Jack sounded uncertain. "But your fingers—"

"Are fine." Ava waved his concern away.

"We could ask the others to come and help."

"No. We need to be quick. The coast is clear now. Seven of us will attract attention. I just want to take a peek." Ava looked down the road. "We'll call them if we need help."

"OK. Where do you want me to stand?" Jack whispered as they scurried to the door of Arch 645.

"There." Ava moved him into position. "Stand with your feet hip width apart. Lean against the brick wall when I step up onto your shoulders. OK?"

"OK." Jack bent his knees and cupped his hands.

"When you feel my weight in your hands" – Ava lifted her foot – "I want you to power into the ground through your feet and push me up." She paused to make sure he understood. "As soon as you feel my weight lift, you need to straighten your legs and lean into the wall, guiding my feet onto your shoulders, then support my ankles."

"Got it." Jack grinned nervously at her. "Then we could run away and join a circus!"

But Ava couldn't respond – she was too worried about Rae. "Are you ready?"

Jack nodded, the expression on his face suddenly concentrated.

Bending her standing leg, Ava hopped up and hissed, "Now!"

Boosted by Jack, Ava was able to grasp the top of the girder. Ignoring the pain in her fingers, she slid her palms flat and pushed herself higher, locking her elbows. Her arms started to tremble. She was tired from her rooftop run. She felt Jack grab her ankles and guide her feet onto his shoulders. Ava lowered herself onto her forearms, allowing Jack to take some of her weight. Pressing her face to the glass, she peered inside.

At first, she only made out dark shapes. The grey daylight that managed to shine through the dirty glass only lit up the foreground. The walls of the arch were lined with gunmetal-grey shelving units, stuffed with boxes and bags. In the middle was an empty expanse of concrete where Ava guessed a vehicle sometimes parked.

Letting Jack take all her weight, Ava cupped her hands around her eyes to see better. There was an odd shape on the top shelf closest to her. It looked like a rhinoceros's head. On the floor below it stood stacks of paintings. The place was a storage facility. A dim glow shone at the back of the arch. It backlit the bars of a cage, as big as one you'd see in a zoo. Inside it, sitting on the floor cross-legged beside a small candle, was the silhouette of Rae.

They had put Rae in a cage!

Ava was shocked. She'd guessed the girl was in some kind of trouble, but nothing like this. Her shock turned to anger and, without thinking, she banged on the glass with her fist.

Rae jumped to her feet. A darkness materialized on her shoulder: Caliban. She saw Ava at the window and looked horrified. She swiped her hand and shouted, "Go away!"

"We want to help you," Ava called through the glass.

Rae shook her head emphatically, waving her hands, indicating that Ava should leave.

"Ava!" Jack's voice was strained with the effort of holding her up. "There's a van turning into the lane. Someone's coming. *Get down!*"

Ava pushed down on the iron girder with her gloved palms, swiftly lifted her legs from Jack's shoulders and dropped to the ground. The pair scurried back along the lane and ducked down behind a vehicle parked outside the mechanic's.

"They've locked her in a cage!" A tremor of anger shook Ava's body. "I saw her, Jack. Rae's in a cage! She's a prisoner!"

A battered white van with *PESTOKIL* written on the side slowed to a stop in front of Arch 645. Two middle-aged men were sitting in the front. The driver was balding, with jowls like a pug. The passenger was a silver-haired, suntanned man, wearing a shiny grey suit with wide lapels over a white T-shirt. A chunky gold chain hung around his neck.

The pug-faced man got out of the van and unlocked the blue shutter, pushing it up. Ava and Jack shuffled forwards as daylight lit up the far wall of the arch.

"What is that?" Jack was squinting. "Is that ivory?"

Ava was only interested in getting a clear view of Rae. The girl had retreated to the back of the cage and had her hand up, blocking the dazzling light. Caliban was croaking angrily.

The pug-faced man returned to the van, driving it into the vacant space in the middle of the arch. The silver-haired man got out. He had a newspaper in his hand and was chortling.

"Baz," he said to the pug-faced man. "The fuzz are saying they think a group *like* the Dead Zoo Gang could be behind the Swan Museum robbery." His mouth split, revealing braces on his teeth; his eyes didn't smile one bit. "But it couldn't have been us, could it, Baz?"

"Reckon it could've been us." Baz cackled, then coughed. "Problem is, Boss, on that particular morning, you was in court for a driving infringement and I drove you there on account of you having your licence taken away. That's what the police call an ironclad alibi." He made a sound like a grunting warthog and Ava realized it was laughter.

"Good thing they don't know about the newest member of our gang, eh?" The silver-haired man turned to the cage in the corner. "You're really part of the family now, Rae, aren't you, my girl?"

"Yeah. Part of the family." The pug-faced man grabbed the shutter and, with a clatter, yanked it down.

20

RUFFLED FEATHERS

As the shutter door touched the ground, Jack nudged Ava. "Let's go," he whispered.

"But Rae…" Ava didn't want to leave the caged girl.

"We can't help her right now. We need the others," Jack insisted. "They're waiting for us at the station."

Ava relented, following Jack down the lane. As they passed under a railway bridge, Ava recognized the road that led to the train station, and they jogged all the way there. Her sister and the others were standing outside on the station steps, looking anxious. When she spotted Ava, Tippi bounced up and down, waving frantically.

"I knew you'd be all right," she gushed, as Ava and Jack ran to meet them. "Oh! Ava!" She pointed. "You're bleeding!"

"That's dried blood, from earlier. I'm fine, Tippi, really, I am."

"What happened?" Tara looked concerned.

"Caliban attacked me." Seeing the look of confusion on their faces, Ava explained. "The raven is called Caliban."

"The raven attacked you?" Twitch looked intrigued.

"Rae told it to," Jack said.

"She ordered the bird to attack you?" Ozuru looked horrified.

"*Listen!*" Ava raised her voice to stop the questions. "We'll tell you everything in a minute." She looked behind her and then at Jack. "We need to go somewhere a bit more private. We need to make a plan."

"Ava's right," Jack said. "It's not safe to talk here."

"Let's talk on the train home," Tara suggested forcefully.

"But..." Ava wanted to do something to help Rae.

"Ava!" Tara stopped her. "We promised my parents we'd be back in time for dinner. You have a wound on your forehead that needs dressing and what did you do to your hands? They're a mess!"

"It's just my fingers." Ava curled her fists and looked pleadingly at Jack. "We can't leave her there, in that cage."

"Who is in a cage?" Tippi asked.

"Let's get on the train," Jack said, trying to herd her towards the station. "There's nothing you or I can do to help Rae right now. She told you that herself. The best thing we can do is take some time to think everything through and make a good plan…"

"To rescue her," Ava insisted.

"Um, guys, you said it wasn't safe to stand around talking about this." Terry lifted his hands and looked around. "Shall we go into the station?"

"Yes," Tara said firmly, taking Tippi's hand. "Come on."

Ava didn't move. She couldn't leave. The image of Rae and Caliban in the giant cage was seared into her mind. She thought of the picture of the innocent, smiling girl Rae had been two years ago. The Dead Zoo Gang had turned her into a criminal. Turning to Jack, she caught him and Twitch using sign language. "What are you two talking about?"

"Nothing." Jack blushed and Ava knew they were talking about her. "Are you OK?"

"Will everyone stop asking me that!" Ava snapped, storming up the station steps. "I'm not the one in a damn cage."

"Next train is in nine minutes," Ozuru told her as the Twitchers gathered around a bench at the end of the platform.

"Sit down," Tara said to Ava. "Ozuru, will you take a look at her hands, please, and the cut on her head."

Ozuru gently placed one of Ava's hands on his knee, studying the welts on her fingers as she told everyone how she'd got them. He looked at Tara. "Ouch!"

"What do you think she should do?" Tara prompted.

"Not slide down any more ladders?" Ozuru shrugged.

"How should she treat her injuries?" Tara asked.

"I don't know."

"But your dad's a doctor!"

"And your dad's an accountant," Terry said, "but you're not brilliant at maths."

"I'm better than you," Tara retorted.

Ava withdrew her hands. She didn't like people fussing over her.

"Let me look," Twitch said, taking Ava's hand before she could put it in her pocket. "When we get on the train, you're going to need to take those gloves off and wash your hands in the bathroom. The blistering will go down quickly, but you see here, where your skin has torn, on your knuckles? There's dirt and rust in there. You need to flush it out. Once it's clean, I'll whack a bit of antiseptic cream on and bandage it up." He pointed to a pocket in his camo trousers. "I've got some with me. Tonight, take the bandages off and let the air get to your cuts." He smiled and Ava found herself smiling back. Twitch had a way of calming her down. "You might want to wear a plaster tomorrow to protect your knuckles, but you'll be fine."

"Thanks."

"Train!" Tippi called out, and everyone except Ava stood up as the engine glided to a stop in front of them.

"We're going to help Rae," Jack told her softly. "But we need to be smart about it, or else she and Caliban could get hurt."

Remembering what Jasper had said about wringing the raven's neck and drowning Rae in the river, Ava nodded, standing up and letting Jack guide her onto the train.

"Can I ask you about the raven?" Twitch said, sitting down beside her, while the others squeezed into a quartet across the aisle. "I'm really curious."

"Caliban can talk," Ava told him. "Did you know ravens could talk? I didn't."

"Talk? Really?"

"I heard him say his own name."

"You said Rae told the raven to attack you?"

"Rae pointed at me, shouted 'Attack!', and Caliban went for me. He pecked my ear and head and pulled out some of my hair! That's why I slid down the ladder. I would've climbed down, but Caliban kept coming at me."

"Fascinating," Twitch said. "Um, I mean, that must've been awful."

Jack was standing in the aisle, telling the others about the railway arch.

"The Dead Zoo Gang!" Terry whistled. "That's a pretty hardcore name."

"I wouldn't normally say this," Jack said. "But this case might be too big for the Twitchers. This isn't about a girl stealing bird skins from a museum. The men we saw are hardened criminals. And I don't think they run a pest control business. I think that's a front. There were bags and boxes of weird-looking stuff in that arch. It was an Aladdin's cave of antiquities and strange stuff. I think we've uncovered the place they store their loot."

"There's a big cage at the back of the arch," Ava added. "Rae and Caliban were locked inside it." She felt a flush of guilt at the horrified expression on Tippi's face, but she knew that her little sister was tough. She would want to help Rae. "The men from the fishing conference were there," Ava said to Ozuru. "You were right, Tara, the blond one is called Jasper. The muscly one is called Phil. He didn't say much. He was trying to get Jasper to stop being horrible about Rae, but he did say that she was their cousin."

There was a gasp at this revelation.

"They must be brothers," Ozuru said, "or possibly cousins."

"We saw another two, older men," Jack said. "I think the one wearing a fancy suit was the boss of the gang. The bloke driving the van was called Baz."

"These are dangerous men," Ava said. "We've got to get Rae away from them."

"But..." Tara paused. "If she's related to them, if they're family... What if she doesn't want to be rescued?"

"She does," Tippi said. "She has a diary called *Escape Plan*."

"She set her raven on you," Terry reminded Ava.

"She was scared," Ava replied. "We broke into her shed."

"We need to think about the right way to handle this." Jack's voice was sombre. "You all know how much I like to solve cases, but I think we should tell the police what's in that arch."

"Yes," Tara agreed immediately.

"No," said Ava at exactly the same time.

"If the police go there," Tippi said, "won't Rae get arrested and sent to prison for stealing the bird skins?" There was silence. "If Rae goes to prison, who will look after Caliban?"

"You mustn't worry, Tippi," Tara said. "I'm sure they won't send Rae to prison."

"Who will look after her then?" Tippi narrowed her eyes. "She's an orphan."

"They will definitely take the bird away," Twitch muttered.

"We're not going to the police," Ava said flatly, crossing her arms. "I won't make Rae's life worse than it already is. She asked me to swear not to talk to the police when we were on the rooftop."

"Did you?" Ozuru asked.

"No, but I should have. If I had she might not have set Caliban on me. Anyway, there's no point in going to the police. They won't listen. Don't you remember what Chief Superintendent Stickler said? He hates kids playing at being detectives. He threw our clues back in our faces. What makes you think they'll even go to the railway arch? They'll just tell us to go home and play with our toys." She got to her feet and looked at Twitch. "I'm going to the bathroom to wash my hands."

"I'll tape them up for you when you get back," he replied.

The Twitchers were still arguing about what they should do when the train pulled in to Briddvale Station.

"Look. We've got a welcoming committee." Terry pointed. "It's Medusa herself!"

Pam was sitting on the platform bench in her pink puffer coat, with a face like thunder. She got up as they disembarked. "Well, if it isn't the intrepid Twitchers, detectives extraordinaire." Her voice was dripping with sarcasm.

"Hi, Pam," Ozuru said.

"Don't you 'hi, Pam' me!" Her nostrils flared as she tossed her hair over her shoulder with an angry flick of her head. "You went looking for Rae Rackem without me!" She glared at each one of them in turn. "You wouldn't even know about her if it wasn't for me! I found her. Not you. I didn't *have* to tell you, but I did. I thought I was an *honorary Twitcher* and we were doing this together." She was shouting. "You were just using me!"

"We really weren't—" Tara started to say.

"I'm not listening to you!" Pam covered her ears. "You're all mean! And I don't care! Do you know what I've been doing today?" She didn't pause long enough to let anyone answer. "I've been making a video about Rae being the thief behind the feather heist. I'm going to upload it to my channel tonight and blow this case wide open. I'm going to take full credit for solving it all on my own." She stalked away up the platform, fuming. "I just came here to tell you that!"

"No! *Pam!*" Ava called out, alarmed.

"I'll go after her," Jack said, sprinting away. "Leave Pam to me."

"I feel bad," Tara said.

Ozuru nodded.

"How long do you think she sat here waiting for us?" Terry chuckled.

"We can't let her upload that video," Ava said to Twitch. "It'll make the Dead Zoo Gang angry. They will punish Rae." She thought of Jasper's sneering face and cruel laugh. "They'll hurt her."

21
FLIGHT PLAN

It was still dark when Ava got up. She placed a note for Tara and Tippi on her pillow, explaining where she was going, and silently scooped up the pile of clothes she'd left at the end of her bed last night. She froze as Tippi wriggled on her air bed. Her little sister turned towards her and opened one eye.

"Are you going to rescue Rae and Caliban?" she whispered.

Ava nodded.

"Good." Tippi rolled over and fell back to sleep.

Ava hurried to the bathroom. She was dressed in two minutes. She checked her hands, pleased that her fingers no longer hurt so much. She wrapped plasters around the knuckles of her left hand and tied her hair up in a top knot. Tiptoeing downstairs, Ava grabbed her rucksack and coat, and slipped her feet into her trainers. Unlocking the front door, she snuck out into the dark, momentarily startled when the outside light illuminated the doorstep. She put her gloves on. It was freezing. The first train of the day was at five-seventeen. She planned to be on it.

Breaking into a run, Ava revelled in the icy burn of the frosty air in her throat and the heat in her muscles.

A familiar voice came out of the darkness. "Looks like I owe you five quid."

Two torch beams switched on. Ava saw Twitch and Jack wrapped in coats and scarves, sitting on their bikes, grinning at her, their breath rising like smoke in the darkness.

"I bet Twitch you'd catch the first train back to Swanhurst," Jack admitted, "to rescue Rae."

"You can't stop me."

"Not planning to stop you," Jack said, turning his bike around. "We're coming with you. Twitch is worried about the raven; you're worried about Rae. Who's going to worry about the two of you? Me, that's who." He smiled at Ava. "Hop onto the handlebars and hold on tight."

Ava clambered onto the front of Jack's bike, glad of the grip on her gloves, and propped her feet on the mudguard over the front wheel. The bitter wind chafed her face as they raced along the road, and Ava felt a shot of glee as she realized how lucky she was to have such friends.

Chaining their bikes to the stand at the station, they bought tickets from the machine and hopped onto the train. It was eerily empty.

"So…" Jack looked at Ava expectantly as he rubbed his hands together to warm them up. "What's your plan?"

"Plan?"

"We thought you'd have one." Twitch blinked. "What were you going to do when you got to the railway arch?"

"Improvise," Ava admitted. "I figure Rae and Caliban will be alone in the arch. I mean, I don't know what criminal-type people do, but my guess is they don't get up at six in the morning unless it's to commit a robbery. I hoped they wouldn't be around, and that I'd have time to work something out."

"I'm no good at picking locks, and none of us has the muscles to break a door down" – Jack opened his rucksack – "but I thought this might help." He pulled out a rolled-up rope ladder. "We can climb up to the window in the arch, smash the glass, get in, get Rae out and—"

"And Caliban," Twitch said.

"Yes, and Caliban. We bring them back to the hide and make an anonymous call to the police telling them about the suspicious goings-on in Arch 645 and leave them to deal with the Dead Zoo Gang."

"I like that plan," Ava said. "It sounds simple."

"Where did you get a rope ladder?" Twitch asked.

"It's from the old swing set in my garden. I attached grappling hooks to the carabiners."

"Did you manage to smooth things out with Pam?" Ava asked him.

"I had to do some grovelling and a bit of bargaining, but she agreed not to post the video," Jack replied. "So we'll see."

The closer the train got to Swanhurst, the more nervous Ava felt. She hoped Rae wouldn't be difficult. By five past six, the three of them were making their way under the railway bridge and down the lane towards Arch 645.

"At least we know they won't have a burglar alarm," Jack muttered.

"Do we know that?" Twitch asked.

"They wouldn't want an alarm going off accidentally and attracting the attention of the police, would they?" Jack took a head torch from his pocket and pulled it on as they approached the arch.

"What's that?" Ava pointed to a grey square next to the torch on Jack's headband.

"A camera." Jack sighed. "I had to promise Pam exclusive footage for her documentary to stop her posting that video. I told her about the arch."

"How are we going to get your ladder up there?" Twitch asked, studying the archway.

"Bunk me up, like yesterday, onto your shoulders," Ava said to Jack. "I'll attach the ladder to the girder."

Once Ava was on Jack's shoulders, Twitch handed her the bundled-up ladder. She was looking for a good place to attach it when a tap on the other side of the glass made her jump. She wobbled, dropping the ladder. It clonked Jack on the head.

"What are you doing?" he whispered, sounding panicked as he tried to steady her.

Caliban was on the other side of the glass, his knowing eyes fixed on Ava. He pecked the glass again.

"It's the raven," Ava whispered to the boys. "He's pecking at the glass. I think he recognizes me."

"You're heavy," Jack complained, and Ava realized she wasn't leaning on the girder. Jack was carrying all her weight on his shoulders. "I've got to put you down."

Ava dropped to the ground.

"Rae's in the cage, but Caliban isn't?" Twitch asked.

"I didn't look."

A new noise silenced her. The door beside the big shutter was being unlocked. Ava glanced at Jack and Twitch in alarm. They stared at the door, but it didn't open.

For a long moment, the three of them stood rooted to the spot. Then Twitch leaned forward and pushed. The door swung open with a *creeeaaak!*

Jack grabbed Ava's arm. He looked ready to run, but Twitch was peering in.

"There's no one here," he told them in a hushed voice, stepping inside.

"Come back," Jack hissed. "Who do you think opened the door? A ghost? It's a trap!"

Ava's heart was thumping. She heard a gurgling *caw* and shook off Jack's hand. "Caliban," she called softly into the darkness.

"Caliban," came a croaked reply.

Ava pushed the door wide open to let in the dingy yellow light of the streetlamps. The van was gone, and perching on the shelves in front of them was the raven.

"Who's there?" came a sleepy voice.

"Rae?" Ava hurried to the cage, kneeling down. "My name is Ava. I'm here with my friends, Jack and Twitch. And before you shout at me, can I just say" – she put her hand over her heart – "I swear on my life that I will

200

never talk to the police about you, or this place, unless you give me permission. Caliban can peck out my eyeballs if I do."

"What are you doing here?" Rae was sitting up on a mattress on the floor of the cage, looking confused. Behind her was an electric radiator, exuding heat. "How did you get in? What time is it?"

"Caliban unlocked the door," Twitch told her.

"We're here to help you escape. I know you think no one can help you" – Ava's words poured out in a rush – "but nobody should be locked in a cage! It's inhuman, and—"

Rae leaned forward, pushing at the cage door. It swung open.

"Oh!" Stunned, Ava didn't know what to say. "It's not locked?"

"Jasper locked it, but it's not the punishment he thinks it is. I like sleeping here," Rae said. "Uncle Tony won't let me bring Caliban into his house. This cage is Caliban's enclosure." She clicked her tongue against the roof of her mouth twice and the raven flew to her.

"How come it's not locked now?" Ava asked.

"We can pick locks," she admitted, ruffling Caliban's neck feathers with the tip of her finger as she studied the three of them. "How did you find this place?"

"Followed you through the tunnel," Jack told her.

Rae looked crestfallen. "I'm going to be in trouble."

"We haven't told anyone," Ava assured her. "No one even knows we're here … well, except my little sister and my best friend, but they won't tell."

"You should go," Rae said. "You don't know what you're getting mixed up in."

"We want to help you," Ava told her.

"Both of you," Twitch added, looking at Caliban.

"I tried to tell you yesterday, on the roof." Rae shook her head. "No one can help me."

"Are you happy, living like this?" Ava asked. "Sleeping in a damp railway arch, in a cage?"

"Happy?" Rae stared up at her with mournful eyes and Ava immediately regretted her question.

"What about school?" Jack asked, changing the subject. "Do you go to school?"

"Yeah. Sometimes. Uncle Tony travels a lot."

"Do you have friends?" Jack asked.

"I have Caliban."

"Why do you think Caliban let us in?" Twitch asked her.

Rae didn't have an answer. She looked lost.

"Maybe he thinks you should have human friends too," Twitch suggested.

"What do you know about birds?" Rae snapped.

"I have chickens and pigeons," Twitch said. "I reared two of the pigeons to be homing birds. They're called Squeaker and Frazzle, and their parents are Scabby and Maude."

"You have birds?" The guarded expression that hooded Rae's eyes lifted.

"They're not really mine. Birds are free creatures. Well, except for my chickens, but yes, I give the birds a home." Twitch smiled at Caliban. "My pigeons look like clowns next to Caliban, though. He's a stunner. I've never seen a bird so clever."

Rae looked at the raven adoringly. "Boop boop," she said softly to the bird.

"Boop boop," Caliban replied.

"Listen, Rae." Ava tried to match Twitch's calm and relaxed manner. "There was a time when I had no parents. My dad died and then my mum was put in prison. It was bad. But I had a nan to take care of me, and a little sister to be strong for. Otherwise..." Ava shrugged. "I probably would've curled up in a ball and never got up again. I know you think—"

"I can't leave," Rae told her calmly.

"You can. We'll help."

"You don't understand. If I run away, my cousin Jasper will kill Caliban."

"Not if they don't know where you and Caliban are," Jack said.

"You're not listening." Rae sat up on her knees. "Jasper has strapped a GPS tracker to Caliban's back. It links to his phone. He did it after I tried to run away once. He knows I never go anywhere without Caliban, and he can see where Caliban is at all times, and … and … if I don't do as they say" – her voice cracked – "he will shoot an electric shock through Caliban's body and kill him dead."

All the air went out of Ava's lungs as she finally understood Rae's predicament.

"I won't do anything to hurt Caliban."

Twitch peered at the raven. "Where's the tracker?"

"The harness goes around his neck. The tracker sits on his back, between his wings. It's black so it's hard to see."

"Have you ever tried to get it off?"

Rae shook her head. "I daren't."

Twitch put his hand into his pocket and then held it out flat, revealing a little brown disc. "Caliban, are you hungry?" He turned his head away so that he wasn't looking at the bird.

"He won't eat…" Rae started to say, but the raven had hopped onto Twitch's hand. He grabbed the brown disc and flew back to Rae's lap to eat it. She looked surprised.

"Was that good, Caliban?" Twitch nodded his head, mimicking the bird's movement. "Want another one?" He opened his hand again, displaying two brown discs this time. He looked away again.

"What are they?" Ava asked as Caliban landed on Twitch's wrist and ate the first and then the second morsel of food.

"Dog food," Twitch said. "Crows love it, so I figured ravens might too. I brought a pocketful." He looked at Rae. "If it's all right with you, I'd like to look at that tracker. I know quite a bit about them. I volunteer at a local bird charity that monitors and collects data from migrating birds like the swallow."

Rae shuffled closer to Twitch. "You really do understand birds?"

"Yes, but I've never had a relationship with a bird like the bond you have with Caliban. To be honest, I'm a bit jealous."

Rae smiled at this, and it was the innocent smile from the newspaper photo. "I am very lucky to have Caliban."

Ava and Jack drew back, letting Twitch and Rae explore Caliban's tracker.

"Look." Jack lifted the corner of a fur pelt draped over a pile on a shelf. "This whole place is full of stolen gear." He tucked his chin so that the camera on his head was pointed at the shelves, and shuffled sideways to capture a good shot for Pam.

"We should see if we can find the bird skins," Ava whispered, glancing back at Rae and Twitch. "Dr Nutt says they must be returned intact with their scientific labels to go back into the collection."

"Check this out!" Jack was standing in front of a clothing rail. "Look at these. There's a police officer's uniform, pest control overalls, a cleaner's smock, security high vis." He pointed the camera as he flicked through them. "I'll bet they use these when they're casing a joint, or robbing it."

Ava looked at the shelves of incriminating evidence and realized just how dangerous it was for them to be here. As she searched for the stolen bird skins, she pulled at a horn-shaped thing. It had a label written in French. "Urgh!" She pushed it back.

"What is it?" Jack came to her side.

"I think that's an elephant tusk!"

Jack bent down and opened the door of a cabinet. "Hey look," he said, taking out a bottle. "Rum! And there's a fancy decanter – I think it's whisky – and four crystal glasses. Bet they've got a poker deck in here somewhere."

"What are we going to do about Rae?" Ava asked as she scanned the shelves for bird skins.

"Breaking and entering tools," Jack exclaimed excitedly as he rummaged through the shelves like an elderly lady at a jumble sale. "I'm getting good evidence. Whoa!" He was lifting a flap of tarpaulin. "That is a lot of cans of petrol!" He wrinkled his nose. "It stinks."

"Jack, we need to make a plan. Time is ticking," Ava said. "We don't want to get caught in here."

"Calm down. It's still dark outside." He reached towards an antique tea chest and carefully opened the lid. "What is that?" He pointed the camera into the crate. "This looks like the canisters of poison used for pest control."

"Stop filming, Jack!" Ava grabbed his arm. "We need to find those bird skins, and work out what to do about Rae."

They looked over at Twitch. Rae was holding Caliban while he studied the tracker on the raven's back. "It looks like an ordinary backpack tracker," Twitch was saying.

"What are we going to do?" Ava whispered.

"I don't know," Jack admitted. "Rae won't come with us in case Caliban is killed. If we find the bird skins, we can't take them because then Rae might be … you know, killed. We can't tell the police what's going on because Rae could end up in prison…"

"And I promised."

Jack threw up his hands. "It's tricky."

"I know." Ava grimaced. "And we're running out of time."

22

CAW-TION!

"Rae," Jack said, spinning around, "about the bird skins you took…" Ava saw Rae's eyes dart to a set of shelves on the other side of the room. "The museum really needs them back."

"I don't know what you're talking about," Rae said, her face becoming a blank mask.

"We know you took them," Ava said. Rae glanced at the shelves a second time. "You and Caliban pulled off the robbery together. It took us a while to work it out."

"Work what out?" Rae said belligerently.

"You came into the museum with my class," Ava told her. "You waited for Caliban by the Darwin display. He pulled the rubber seal from the toilet window and flew to you, keeping high so as not to be seen. You know how to pick locks, but you didn't. You put a lock picking tool into the door handle and placed a rock for Caliban to smash the glass, to make it look like an attempted robbery. This was the decoy. You and Caliban then went up in the lift to level three, to the Wallace Room. Caliban opened the door for you, after learning the code by watching staff key it in through the window opposite. You emptied the drawers into two bin bags, sent the raven back down to the Darwin case, whistled to signal he should set off the alarm by smashing it with the rock. Then you caught the lift down to the lower ground floor, snuck to the toilets, slipped out of the broken window, hid the bird skins in that hole in the woods, and made your way round to the bus stop, where I met you."

Rae blinked but said nothing.

"Did we mention, we're detectives?" Jack did a little bow.

"Ava," Twitch said. "Ravens are clever, but I don't think even Caliban…"

"No." Rae stopped him. "She's right. Well. Almost right. I knew the code to the door because Caliban showed it to me. He can memorize patterns." She moved the bedding aside and Ava saw an odd assortment of bric-a-brac, a bottle top, a shell, a pinecone, a golf ball, and a keypad with numbers zero to nine on it, like the one that opened the lock on the Wallace Room door.

"These are Caliban's toys." Rae picked up the keypad and clicked her tongue against the top of her mouth twice. "Caliban numbers." She double-clicked her tongue against the top of her mouth again. "Caliban numbers."

The raven hopped up to her wrist and pecked at numbers two, two, six, nine.

"Good boy, Caliban," cooed Rae, rubbing the top of his head. "Boop boop."

"Boop boop," replied the raven.

"Weeks ago, I sent Caliban up to the window to watch the door. I'd trained him using this. When someone punched the code in, and he saw the numbers, he flew down and showed me the key code. When the coast was clear, I then went and tested that it worked."

"That's amazing," Twitch whispered.

"That's criminal," Jack said, sounding impressed.

Rae's shoulders slumped. "It was like Ava said," she admitted, "except when I met Caliban by the Darwin case and gave him his rock. He stayed there, hidden on the beam above it. I went to the Wallace Room and opened the door. No one was around. I filled a bag with the dead birds as quickly as I could, but, I've never stolen anything before. I got frightened. I was scared someone might spot Caliban. I have a whistle." She reached into the neck of her top and pulled out a chain with a small silver whistle hanging from it. "I blew it, to signal Caliban should trigger the alarm and come to me. He threw the stone and flew up to the Wallace Room. I shoved the last few birds into a bag and came down in the lift with him. The rest you got right. Caliban stood guard whilst I hid the birds in that hole." She hung her head in shame.

"None of that matters to us," Ava told her. "We've sworn not to tell a soul and we keep our promises. The thing we need to know is, do you *want* to be a member of the Dead Zoo Gang or not?"

"No." Rae shook her head. "But I don't have any choice. I've committed a crime now. I'm like them. If I'm caught, I'll go to prison. Uncle Tony says…"

"You are not like them," Ava insisted. "Did you plan the robbery?"

"No."

"Did you want to do it?"

"No, but, Jasper gets so angry. He said I was a dead weight and a liability and Uncle Tony said I had to prove I wasn't…"

"Rae, you're a child who was made to commit a crime. If you really want to escape, then we are going to help you. That's a promise."

"I do." Rae's reply was a whisper. "But I can't."

Suddenly Caliban let out a deep, rasping call. He turned his head to Rae and snapped his beak together several times. Rae jumped up. Caliban flapped around her head. "You've got to get out of here! They're coming!"

"Who's coming?" Twitch asked.

"My cousins. Caliban can hear their car." She herded them out of the cage. "Quick! You've got to go. *NOW!*"

Ava jumped up. The black bags that she suspected contained the bird skins were only a couple of metres away. It would only take a second to check. Jack saw her move towards the shelves. He pointed to the petrol cans under the tarpaulin. "Rae, why is there so much petrol here?" he asked, diverting her attention.

Ava darted to the black bags on the shelf, pulled back the plastic, and glimpsed yellow and orange feathers. It was the missing birds.

"Jasper likes to burn things," Rae was saying as she shoved Jack towards the door. "You've got to get out of here!" She pushed him and Twitch through, shut it, and locked it.

Turning around, Rae saw Ava and her eyes grew wide. They both heard the roar of an approaching engine.

"Get in the cage." Rae ran towards it. "You've got

to hide!" She yanked Ava inside, pulling the cage door shut behind her. "If they catch you in here, they'll kill you." Rae kicked her mattress into the furthest corner of the cage. "Lie down," she ordered.

Ava dropped onto the mattress, her heart galloping. Rae covered her with the sleeping bag.

"Don't move!" Rae whispered, lying down on the mattress in front of Ava, wriggling under a bit of the sleeping bag.

Ava listened. There were no shouts or sounds that might suggest Jack and Twitch had been caught outside the arch. She heard the rattle of the shutter door rising, the ostentatious purr of the black sports car as it drove inside. Someone walked in behind it and closed the shutter door.

"They won't come in the cage," Rae whispered. "They're scared of Caliban."

Through a tiny chink in the covers, Ava saw the raven perching on a stick above her head.

A car door opened. She heard approaching footsteps. She held her breath. Rae's breathing was deep and regular. She was pretending to be asleep.

Ava worked through what she would do if she was discovered. It was three against two if you counted Caliban, and she did. It occurred to her that the elephant tusk might make a good weapon, and she had the element of surprise, her gymnastics, and Caliban's claws and beak. She wondered if Rae was any good in a fight.

The footsteps moved away. Ava glimpsed Jasper's hair. What was he doing? Had there been another robbery? Had they come to stash some loot? She suppressed a shiver of fear. She mustn't move.

"Are we meeting Dad?" the low voice of Phil asked.

"At eight. We're early. I just needed to do something." Ava heard the chink of glass. She shifted slightly, trying to see. Jasper was by the drinks cabinet with his back to her.

"Are you putting the kettle on?" Phil asked, moving towards his brother.

"There's no milk," Jasper said, turning around with a cold, calculating smile on his face. "Why don't we go and get some coffee from the station cafe? We can leave the car here."

"I could do with a bacon butty." Phil nodded enthusiastically.

"Let's go," Jasper said, walking past him. "Come on."

After a long moment of silence, Rae made two clicking noises with her mouth. Caliban made two clicking noises back. Rae threw the sleeping bag off and Ava realized she'd been asking the raven for the all clear.

"You have to get out of here." Rae looked frightened. "Uncle Tony could walk through that door any minute."

"I'm going." Ava dashed over to the place where Jasper had been standing, in front of the drinks cabinet. What had he been doing? She saw a kettle clogged with limescale on a grubby tray. Beside it was a bowl of sugar cubes, two empty glasses that could do with a clean – one had plastic spoons in – and a dirty mug with fur growing in it.

"Ava! You're not listening to me." Rae was out of the cage and over by the door. "If you don't go, we'll both end up dead."

Ava snatched out her phone and snapped a series of photos of the shelves in front of her. Jasper had done something there – she was certain of it. He'd checked Rae was asleep before doing it. But what was it?

"Ava!"

"Coming." Ava ran to Rae. "You've got to come with us."

"I won't leave Caliban." She opened the door and peered out, checking the coast was clear. "Don't worry about me. I know how to deal with Uncle Tony, and he knows how to deal with Jasper." The determined look on Rae's face told Ava this wasn't an argument she could win.

"Wait." Ava pulled out her casebook and pen and scribbled down her phone number. She hesitated for a second, then added, *Briddvale, Aves Wood*. "This is my number, and this" – she pointed to the words – "is where we have a secret hideout. No one knows about it. You would be safe there. If you need us—"

"Thanks." Rae snatched the paper and shoved Ava out into the lane. She flashed her an apologetic smile. "I mean it. Thanks."

The door closed. Ava heard it lock.

23
FOILED

"Pssstttt!" Jack and Twitch's heads popped up from behind a car outside the mechanic's arch, and Ava felt a rush of relief to see her friends.

"Are you OK?" Twitch asked, wide-eyed, as she ran over to them.

"I hid in the cage." She squatted down between them and the three of them huddled together. "They didn't see me. They're coming back in half an hour to meet Uncle Tony, the big boss." Ava realized that she was shaking. "I found the bird skins – they're in those two black bags on the shelves opposite the cage."

"We should call the police," Jack said.

"No," Ava said, vehemently. "I swore to Rae we wouldn't. We need to get her and Caliban out of there first."

"I think I can get it off." Twitch looked at Ava and

Jack. "Caliban's tracker. I took a look at it, and I've thought of a way to remove it."

"How?" Ava and Jack asked at the same time.

"If the tracker is rigged up to zap Caliban, it must be sending a low current of electricity through the bird to create a circuit. If the circuit is broken – by lifting if away from the bird's back – then it will deliver an electric shock. To do this, there must be the electrodes that create the circuit, and a separate electrode to deliver the shock, which is probably hooked up to the neck harness. A shock around the neck would kill him."

"Horrible," Ava muttered.

"But, if I get a bit of foil, say from a KitKat wrapper" – he pulled a balled-up wrapper from his coat pocket – "roll it and make it into a loop, I could hold it against the two electrodes, to keep the circuit live. Then, hypothetically, I should be able to undo the neck band and slip the whole thing off, without triggering the shock."

"Rae could leave!" Ava's spirits lifted.

"Wait, but what if that doesn't work?" Jack asked.

"I've thought of that," Twitch said. "If I pinch the end of the third electrode as I lift, then if there is a shock, I'll take it into my body."

"Won't that hurt?"

"Probably," Twitch admitted, "but Rae and Caliban would be free."

"Then what are we waiting for?" Ava jumped up just as a large white van with *PESTOKIL* written on the side turned into the lane. She dropped back down. "Uncle Tony's here!"

"We'll wait until the Dead Zoo Gang is gone," Twitch said under his breath as they watched the van approach, "then free Caliban and Rae, grab the bird skins, and take them all back to the hide."

"And then?" Jack asked.

"We call the police with a mysterious tip-off about the Dead Zoo Gang's railway arch," Ava said, "and return the birds to the museum."

"What about Rae and Caliban's part in the theft?" Twitch asked.

"I'm not breaking my promise to her," Ava replied.

They watched in silence as the pug-faced man got out of the van and opened the shutter. "Bleedin' heck," he muttered, shaking his head when he saw Jasper's car. He went into the arch then came back out. "Your boy's parked his motor in the arch and gone off," he told Tony through the open window. "Thought you told him he had to park out here?"

"I did, Baz." Tony did not look happy. "I'll get him

to move the car when he comes back." The van door opened and he stepped down.

Baz looked down the lane. "There's no sign of him."

"Phil will bring him."

Tony strolled into the arch while Baz parked the van. Slipping her binoculars from her rucksack, Ava spied on him. Rae was back on her mattress, pretending to be asleep. Baz went into the arch and the shutter came down.

"I don't trust Jasper," Ava whispered. "He's up to something."

"What d'you mean?" Jack asked.

"When I was hiding in the cage, he checked Rae was asleep while Phil was closing the shutter, then he went over to the drinks station and, thinking no one was watching, he did something."

"What did he do?"

"I don't know," Ava admitted, "but he wasn't fixing himself a drink. Phil seemed confused that they were half an hour early for the meeting with their dad. Jasper deflected Phil's questions by suggesting they go and get coffee from the station cafe."

"I wonder what he was doing?" Jack looked intrigued.

"I got a couple of pictures of the area Jasper was facing." Ava handed her phone to him. "I couldn't see anything obvious, but you might."

"Here they come," Twitch whispered.

"Wonder what new job Dad has for us?" Phil was saying as the two men approached the arch carrying a cardboard tray with four takeaway coffee cups in it.

"Probably some piddling old collection in a decrepit manor house somewhere," Jasper muttered with disgust. "The man has no ambition."

"I like those jobs. They're nice and safe."

"You and Dad are like two peas in a pod," Jasper said in a scathing mutter.

"Aw, thanks." Phil smiled, taking this to be a compliment.

Jasper shook his head as he followed his brother through the door into Arch 645.

Ava, Twitch and Jack all stared at the arch, straining their ears.

"Well now, what are you three up to?" came a man's voice from behind them.

It was all Ava could do to stop herself from screaming as her heart almost exploded out of her chest.

"Morning," Twitch said cheerfully. He raised his binoculars. "We're birdwatching."

The man, who was wearing blue overalls marked with grease, looked amused. He lifted his eyes to the railway bridge. "Seen anything good?"

"Nothing out of the ordinary," Twitch said. "A robin, some pigeons."

"We're searching for the lilac roller that was on the news," Jack said. "It's very rare."

"A lilac roller, eh? Never heard of it," the mechanic said. "Doesn't sound like a local bird."

"Oh, it's not," Twitch said, producing his field guide. "This is what it looks like."

"I hope you don't mind us sheltering behind the car," Jack said. "It's cold this morning. The car makes a good windbreak."

"I'm afraid I've got to move it into the garage, to give it a service." He tossed the keys up and caught them. "Sorry."

The three of them got to their feet. Ava found her legs were stiff. She folded forwards, wrapping her hands around her heels to stretch out her hamstrings. As the car reversed up the lane, they looked about for a new place to hide. Ava felt exposed and vulnerable, standing across from Arch 645. "What do we do now?"

"We could hide behind their van," Jack suggested.

"But Tony said he was going to make Jasper move the car," Twitch said.

"Shhhh." Ava thought she heard a raised voice. There was a crashing sound. She looked at Twitch and Jack in alarm.

"To the hairdresser's," Jack said, grabbing Ava's and Twitch's arms and pulling them to the door of the hairdresser. But the lights were off and the sign on the door said it didn't open till ten.

The door of Arch 645 was flung open. The three of them spun round, pressing themselves up against the glass. Ava found she was holding Jack's hand. She squeezed it tight, her heart in her mouth.

Phil and Baz came out of the arch, each with one of Tony's arms over their shoulders. He appeared to be unconscious. They carried him to the van, Baz opened the passenger door, and Phil lifted Tony in, then got in next to him, holding his head up. Baz ran around to the driver's seat, looking panic-stricken. The doors slammed. The van did a speedy turn in the road, the wheels spun, and it accelerated away down the lane.

Ava stared after it in shocked silence, then a thought hit her. "Rae's alone in there, with Jasper!" She heard a muffled cry as she burst through the door of Arch 645. Jack and Twitch were right behind her. "Rae!"

The girl was lying on the floor, curled up in a protective ball.

Jasper was standing over her, fending off Caliban, who was making shrill alarm calls over and over again as he dive-bombed the blond man's face, claws forward.

At the sound of Ava's voice, Jasper turned. "Who the hell are you?"

"Smile, Jasper!" Jack pointed to the camera on his headband. "You're on camera!"

Jasper lurched towards Jack, who zipped round the black supercar so it was between him and the furious member of the Dead Zoo Gang. Ava realized immediately that he was trying to draw the man away from Rae.

Caliban flew to the shelving unit behind Jasper, gripped the top shelf with his claws and flapped his wings backwards, pulling. Twitch ran to help the bird, yanking the shelf away from the wall, letting it fall. Jasper spun around as the shelves clattered down, hurling antiquities at him, knocking him backwards. His head slammed against the bonnet of his car and he slid to the floor.

Rae moaned and Ava rushed to her side. "Rae, are you OK?"

"He hit me with an ivory tusk."

"He's still breathing," Jack said, cautiously leaning over Jasper who was trapped beneath the shelving unit. "I think he's just unconscious."

"Put your arms around my neck." Ava helped Rae to her feet. "We're getting you out of here."

"Caliban," Rae croaked, seeing Twitch holding the raven in his hands.

Twitch was studying the harness that ran round Caliban's neck. He slid his folded foil under the rectangular tracker, gently working his fingers beneath it. Ava saw him do something imperceptible with his thumbs, and, like a magician's trick, the tracker was suddenly no longer on the bird. Twitch let out a scream, bending double and dropping the unit to the floor.

"You OK?" Jack asked, worried.

"Yeah." Twitch straightened up. "Just a bit shocked." He gave Jack a wry smile.

"That is a terrible joke!" Jack chuckled with relief.

"Everything's going to be all right, Rae," Ava reassured her. "Caliban's tracker is off. You're free."

"We should go." Twitch glanced nervously at Jasper.

"One second," Jack said, moving his head in a slow sweeping motion. "I want to get all of this on camera."

"Where did you say the bird skins are?" Twitch asked Ava.

"There." Ava nodded to the black bags and Twitch ran to the shelves on the other side of the arch, grabbing the two black bin liners and glancing inside. "Bingo!" he said. "Right, let's get out of here before Jasper wakes up!"

24
FEATHERWEIGHT DETECTIVES

Trying to look calm and casual, Jack and Twitch, each with a bin bag slung over their shoulder, sauntered away from Arch 645. Ava followed behind with her arm around Rae's waist, and Caliban flew above them.

"We need to get you to the station and onto a train," Ava told Rae. "Then you'll be safe. It's not far."

"Caliban," Rae mumbled.

"Look up," Ava told her. "He's with us."

The station was busy with mid-morning travellers. Jack led them to the platform for the Briddvale train and Ava saw to her relief that there was a train arriving. They went to the end of the platform and Twitch mimicked the click Rae used to call Caliban. He held out a dog treat, and the raven descended to Twitch's wrist. He curled his fist around the treat and stepped onto the train with Caliban poking his beak into the crack between his fingers, trying to reach the food. Once the doors had closed, Twitch opened his fist flat and let Caliban eat it.

"He trusts you," Rae said, in wonder.

Passengers were staring at the raven. One or two were alarmed enough to move into the next carriage.

"I've messaged the others," Jack said. "They'll be at the station to help."

"Good." Ava looked at him, then Twitch, suddenly aware that they were carrying two bin bags of stolen bird skins worth millions of pounds, in the company of the girl who stole them, and drawing attention to themselves by bringing a raven on the train.

"Twitch, can you take a look at the bump on Rae's head? It looks nasty. She might have concussion." Ava wasn't exactly sure what concussion was, but she knew it was caused by a serious bang to the skull and it could make you sick.

Twitch got up and stood over Rae, parting her hair to peer at an egg-sized lump. "How are you feeling?" he asked her.

"Confused," Rae admitted.

"You're not bleeding, but you're going to have a headache."

Caliban hopped onto Rae's shoulder and rubbed his beak against her cheek. "Boop boop," the bird said.

"Boop boop," Rae replied weakly.

"Are you able to tell us what happened in the arch?" Jack asked her gently.

"An argument. Uncle Tony was angry with Jasper for parking inside." Rae closed her eyes. "Uncle Baz was talking about some painting in a posh house that was worth a lot of money. He wanted Jasper and Phil to steal it. Jasper said that he worked too hard for not enough money, that they should send me to steal the painting, and that he wanted to pull off a big job, like robbing a bank. Uncle Tony told Jasper to pipe down and show Baz some respect. Then" – she paused – "it was weird. Caliban flew out of the cage and did his alarm call at Uncle Tony. I don't know why. Uncle Tony ignored him. Then Caliban mimicked Uncle Tony's voice and called out, 'Jasper! No! Jasper! No!'

"They were all getting cross with Caliban. I tried to call him to me but he flew to the drinks cabinet, picked up a sugar cube from the bowl and threw it at Jasper. He kept doing it. Uncle Baz and Phil started laughing but Jasper was furious. He grabbed the elephant tusk from the shelf and tried to hit Caliban, but Caliban kept throwing sugar cubes at him and calling out his name."

"Jasper hates Caliban, doesn't he?" Ava said, remembering what the man had said about wringing the raven's neck.

"Yes." Rae nodded. "But Caliban hates Jasper more. Every chance he gets, he plays tricks on him. Once, he got a slug in his beak and when Jasper wasn't looking, he hopped into his car and dropped the slug on the driver's seat and hopped out again." A smiled tugged at her lips. "Jasper sat on it. He was not happy. But he couldn't prove that Caliban did it."

"What happened next?" Jack asked, and Ava realized he was taking notes in his casebook.

"Then…" A faraway look came into Rae's eyes. "Uncle Tony was drinking his coffee, and he made a weird jerky movement, spilling it. His hands went to his chest. He fell to his knees, then the ground. Uncle Baz called out his name, throwing down his cup and shouting to Phil as he ripped open Uncle Tony's shirt and started doing CPR. He called to Phil and Jasper to help, but they were both just staring." She shuddered at the memory. "I think Uncle Tony was having a heart attack." She looked at them. "Phil and Uncle Baz took Uncle Tony to the hospital. That's when Jasper turned and hit me with the elephant tusk." She blinked. "I don't remember anything after that. Then you were lifting me up, telling me it was going to be all right." She smiled shyly at Ava. "I guess I was wrong. You did help me after all."

When the four of them and Caliban stepped off the train in Briddvale, the other Twitchers were anxiously waiting.

"Everyone, this is Rae and Caliban," Jack said.

Rae clung to Ava. Caliban, perched on Rae's shoulder, peered inquisitively at the children.

"You did it!" Tippi bounced on her toes, looking proudly at her sister.

"Did you get the bird skins?" Ozuru asked.

"Yes." Twitch held up the two bags.

"Well done," Tara said to Ava. "Although I'm a bit cross you didn't take me with you."

"Sorry." Ava felt a flush of guilt. "I couldn't leave Tippi on her own."

"I know. It's all right." Tara smiled at Rae. "My name's Tara. Welcome to Briddvale."

"And I'm Tippi, but you probably knew that because I'm Ava's sister."

Rae looked overwhelmed to be surrounded by so many excited voices. Caliban took off and circled overhead.

"We've got a lot to tell you." Ava's voice was hoarse and she felt weary from their adventures. "But we can't hang around here. We don't want to draw attention to ourselves."

"Why?" Terry asked.

Jack nodded his head at the black bags and whispered, "We've got millions of pounds of stolen feathers on us."

"Oh yeah." Terry blinked, then looked up and down the empty platform. "We should motor."

"Er, guys?" Pam's voice cut through the hubbub. She was standing back from the group, wearing headphones and holding a small radio. "We've got problems!" She gave Rae an apologetic look as she lifted a headphone off her left ear. "Is Antony Rackem your uncle?"

Rae nodded.

"They're saying he's dead. Did you know that?"

"Dead?" Rae looked blank.

"Oh Rae!" Ava didn't know what to say.

"There's more," Pam said. "Swanhurst police have released a statement saying Antony Rackem's death is suspicious and they're treating it as murder. They're asking anyone with information to come forward. They're looking for you."

"Me? Murder?" Rae looked frightened.

"Yeah." Pam looked around. "I think that makes us all aiders and abettors."

There was a stunned silence.

"Let's go to the hide," Twitch said. "We'll decide what to do once we're there."

As one, they hurried to the exit.

"What about me?" Pam called after them. "You don't want me in your Wendy house. I know you don't."

Ozuru looked at Tara, who looked at Ava, who looked at Jack, who looked at Twitch, who looked at Terry.

"How many times?" Terry huffed. "It's a *hide*, and of course you're coming. But you'll have to develop amnesia afterwards, or, you know, try and be a nicer person."

"I will." Pam looked pleased as she jogged towards them. "I'll delete that video of you doing the—"

"Hup-up-up!" Terry said over the end of her sentence. "Come on, everyone." And he strode off down the platform.

"Don't worry," Tippi said, sliding her hand into Rae's. "We'll take care of you."

Ava and Jack walked at the head of the group. Pam and Tara came to stand either side of Tippi and Rae. Twitch and Ozuru brought up the rear, each carrying a bag of bird skins.

"What I want to know," Jack said to Ava under his breath, "is why the police think Antony Rackem was murdered."

"I don't understand. Rae and her Uncle Baz thought he had a heart attack," Ava said, trying to suppress her alarm. "Do you think we're in trouble?"

"Ava, we're the Twitchers, not the Dead Zoo Gang." Jack smiled reassuringly at her, taking out his keys to unlock his and Twitch's bikes. "We might only be featherweight detectives, but we're the good guys."

25
A FEATHERED NEST

By the time they reached the hide, the energy that had driven Ava all morning was used up. Her body felt heavy and her bones ached. She watched as Tara and Tippi fussed around Rae, drawing her into the triangle room at the back of the hide. Caliban flew into the branches of the tree. To Ava's surprise, the triangle room was stuffed with blankets and cushions.

"When Tippi showed me your note," Tara explained, "I guessed that, if you were successful, you'd bring Rae to the hide." She waved her hand at the welcoming pile of soft furnishings. "So, we brought provisions."

"Provisions?" Ava said, as she crawled into the triangle room, slumping onto the cushions and pulling a blanket over her legs. "Is there food?" She was suddenly starving.

"Yes." Tippi clapped her hands excitedly. "You two sit there and relax." She hurried into the cabin and returned with a giant Thermos. "Have you got the cups, Tara?"

Tippi poured out two tin cups of steaming hot chocolate and presented them to Rae and Ava.

Ava drank deeply and felt the sweet liquid warming her from the inside, soothing her frazzled nerves. "This is heaven in a cup," she said to Tippi, as her little sister clucked happily around them like a mother hen.

"This place is awesome!" Pam said, greedily taking in every detail as Terry gave her the guided tour of the hide. "I didn't spot it when I was walking towards it. It's almost invisible."

Rae watched Jack and Twitch carry the stolen bird skins through to the cabin where they carefully took out a couple and laid them reverently on the table.

"I'm going to cook," Ozuru said, poking his head into the triangle room. "Are you hungry? I'm making scrambled eggs."

"Yes, please." Ava's empty stomach flipped at the thought of food and Rae nodded shyly. "You're safe here," Ava reassured her. "No one knows about this place."

"I can't remember anyone's name," Rae admitted in a quiet voice.

"Ozuru is the one cooking," Ava said, as they watched him building a fire in the stone circle outside the hide.

"He's really good at organizing things and, when we're solving crimes, he's the one who keeps track of clues and suspect interviews. Honestly, without him we'd all be in a muddle most of the time. Then there's Tippi, my little sister." She found herself smiling as Tippi marched round the smoking fire calling instructions to Ozuru. "She's small, but mighty."

"Terry" – Ava pointed up the ladder to the viewing platform where he was showing Pam the pigeon loft – "is Ozuru's best friend. He's a smart-mouthed chatterbox."

"Erm, rude!" Terry poked his head through the ladder hole. "I heard that!" He winked at Rae.

"Pam is an investigative reporter," Ava went on, "not really a detective."

Ava nodded to Tara who was sitting in the entrance to the hide, cracking eggs into a mixing bowl. "Tara is a loyal friend and brave too. I'd trust her with my life."

Tara must've heard because she looked at Ava and smiled.

"And then there's Twitch and Jack … and…" Ava watched Jack studying the labels on the bird skins. He ran his fingers through his hair and it occurred to Ava that she liked watching his mind at work.

"And…?" Rae prompted, an amused look on her face.

"And…" Ava felt herself blushing. "He and Twitch are best friends."

"Twitch is nice," Rae said softly.

"He's a legend. I swear he's the closest thing in real life to a superhero. Either that or he's part bird. He helped me and Tippi when we were in real trouble with the police."

"He did?"

"Yeah. We're not from Briddvale. We don't live here, but we come every holiday because these guys are the best friends you could wish for."

After a moment, Rae said, "I'm not sad about my uncle dying. He wasn't a good person."

Ava wasn't sure how to respond. She felt like she should hug Rae, but she wasn't good at affection, unless it was with Tippi, so she nodded sympathetically. "You don't get to choose your family, but you do get to choose your friends."

Rae smiled and the girls sat in silence, watching the activity around them.

Ozuru presented them with two tin plates heaped with toast, scrambled egg and a healthy puddle of tomato ketchup. Rae wolfed hers down and, as Ava ate, she wondered how often the Dead Zoo Gang fed Rae. Considering how skinny and small she was, Ava doubted it was three times a day.

After another cup of hot chocolate, Rae lay back on the cushions and, within minutes, she was asleep.

Ava covered the girl in blankets, lay down beside her, and closed her eyes. It was a relief to let the warm darkness carry her into slumber.

Ava woke up to find Tippi shaking her gently. She gestured for Ava to come out of the triangle room. Rae was still fast asleep. Ava peeled off the blankets and crawled out, zipping up the tent door to keep the heat in. She shivered as her body adjusted to the temperature drop.

"Sorry to wake you up," Tippi whispered, "but we're having a meeting about what to do and I thought you'd be cross if we let you sleep through it."

"Thanks." Ava nodded. "I would've been."

"We need to work out what we're going to do with the birds … and Rae," Jack was saying as she entered the cabin. "We can't hide in Aves Wood for ever." He smiled at Ava as she sat down on her tree stump. Pam was studying the cabin wall, where they had pinned up things relating to the feather heist case. The list of birds that Rae had used was there, inside the freezer bag, and the black feather that belonged to Caliban.

"Ava, I think we should go over everything that's

happened so far, to make sure we're all up to speed."

Pam nodded, pulling out her phone and turning on her audio recorder.

Ava retold the story of how Rae and Caliban pulled off the feather heist, including the information Rae had told her. Then Jack took over the story of their early morning trip to Arch 645.

"And yes, before you ask, Pam, I filmed everything. I was actually wondering if there's a way to see the footage? There's something I really want to look at."

"I can plug the camera into my phone," Pam said, nodding. "I'm keen to see it too."

"There's something important Ozuru and I need to tell you," Tara said. "We forgot about it in the drama of yesterday, but when we spoke to Rae's neighbours about the house fire, there was a sweet old lady, next door but one, who remembered the night of the fire clearly because, in her words, 'some idiot parked his black sports car across my driveway!'"

Jack leaned forwards, all his attention focused on Tara. "Jasper Rackem has a black sports car!"

"The car stopped her husband from being able to take her to play bridge. The explosion woke her from her sleep. She was one of the people who called the fire brigade, but the sports car was gone by then. I checked."

"Jasper Rackem was at Rae's house on the night of the fire!" Jack whispered.

"The neighbour said it was a miracle Rae survived, but that no one knew what had happened to her. A rumour went around that she had gone to live with her uncle in Swallowsdown. Then," – Tara looked around at them – "and this is the important bit, she told us that a week after the fire a woman had knocked on her door saying she was Rae's mother's cousin. She was searching for Rae. She wanted Rae to know that she had family who cared, but that she was having trouble contacting Tony Rackem." Tara drew breath. "So, perhaps there is some family out there who would want to take care of Rae."

Ava felt a tide of hope. "We need to find that woman."

"It might be better if we clear Rae of murder first," Terry said.

"After Jack told me about them, I did some digging into the Dead Zoo Gang," Pam said, sliding several sheets of paper into the centre of the table. "I found a few articles that mention them. It's speculation, but they talk about how the Rackem family have been linked to the Dead Zoo Gang. It's never been proven that they are a part of it. The Dead Zoo Gang is a name the papers made up," she explained. "After a series of thefts from museums, including a big rhino horn heist, an Irish journalist came up with the name for the thieves."

"I don't get it," Ozuru said. "Why the Dead Zoo Gang?"

"It's a joke name for museums," Terry explained. "People say they're *dead zoos* because they've got cases of stuffed animals instead of cages of living ones."

"Oh!" Ozuru sighed. "It's not a very funny joke."

"It's an accurate name," Ava said, thinking about the case with the stuffed walrus in it.

"Whenever a museum or art gallery is robbed, the papers love to say the Dead Zoo Gang is behind it, but they've never been prosecuted," Pam said. "The Rackems have been brought in for questioning countless times, but they've always got alibis. And these crimes don't just take place in England. They've hit museums all over Europe."

"We don't know that all of them are the Dead Zoo Gang," Tara pointed out.

"No, but some of them definitely are. There are too many coincidences. Like, when the museum in Paris was robbed, Antony Rackem just happened to be in the city having a romantic weekend with his wife." Pam lifted her eyebrows. "She and a waiter in a restaurant provided him with an alibi."

"Last night, when I got home, I looked into *PESTOKIL*," Jack said. "It's the Rackem family business. The company is registered to an address in Swallowsdown and Antony Rackem is listed as the owner. As far as I can tell, he took the business over from his dad."

"They're like the Mafia!" Terry said, looking thrilled.

"Wait, if Tony is Rae's uncle," Tippi said, "does that mean her mum or dad was his brother or sister?"

Ava sat up straight. This hadn't occurred to her.

"Brother, I think," Jack replied. "Rae's dad was Walter Rackem, Tony Rackem's older brother. He's mentioned in the articles about the fire."

"Do you think Rae's dad was involved in the family business?" Ozuru asked, aghast.

"Possibly." Jack looked grave. "Crime does seem to run in her family."

26
WATCHING FOR
A SNOW GOOSE

"Where is Rae going to sleep tonight?" Ozuru asked. "She can't stay with one of us – our parents might recognize her and call the police."

"She could sleep here," Jack suggested.

"On her own?" Ava shook her head.

"It's freezing!" Tara protested.

"It's all right, I'm used to the cold," Rae said, and they all turned. She was standing in the cabin doorway. "And I want to be with Caliban."

"We could all stay here," Ava suggested.

"Yeah!" Terry's face lit up. "We can tell our folks that a rare nocturnal bird is in the woods or something and that we want to camp out together."

"That would work," Jack said, and everyone was nodding. "We just need Twitch to come up with a plausible rare bird that might be spotted in February in Briddvale."

They all looked at Twitch.

"Might I suggest a snow goose?" he said, after a moment's thought. "Snow geese breed in Greenland and Alaska, and normally migrate to North America, but the odd one is spotted in Europe every so often. I'd love to see one."

"Am I allowed to stay too?" Pam asked, tentatively.

"Sure," Terry replied, glancing around to check this was OK. "Why not?"

Pam flushed with pleasure. "Thanks."

"But you will have to take The Twitchers Oath first," Terry added.

"I don't mind," Pam said, surprising them.

"What's The Twitchers Oath?" Rae asked.

"It's an oath we swear to protect birds," Tippi explained, tapping her two fingers against her thumb, using the sign for bird, and launching into it. "I do solemnly swear never to knowingly hurt a bird. I will respect my feathered friends and help them when they are in need. I will protect every bird, be it rare, endangered or common, and fight to conserve their habitats, or may crows peck out my eyes when I'm dead. For I am a Twitcher, now and for ever."

"Oh, I like that!" Rae smiled. "Can I take it too?'

The nine children stood around the hide table and recited the oath together. Ava looked round at everyone's faces as they repeated the words and felt a surge of strength and affection. She hoped Rae felt it too.

"We've a lot to do," Ozuru said as they all sat down again. He tapped his pen against his notebook. "I suggest we divide it up. First, we all need to get permission from our parents to camp out. Then we're going to need air beds, a pump, bedding, warm clothes, hot water bottles…" He reeled off a list. "I've got good camping gear. Who else has stuff that's good for winter camping?"

"I do," Jack said. "I'll get it when I go home."

"I've got some," Twitch nodded.

"We've got three Arctic sleeping bags," Pam said, surprising everyone.

"I don't have camping stuff, but I'm good at carrying things," Terry said.

"I want to go to the library and see what I can find out about the person that old neighbour told us about." Tara glanced at Rae.

"I think you should tell her," Ava said.

"We think your mum had a cousin," Tippi blurted out.

"A cousin?"

"We're not certain," Tara said. "But one of your old neighbours said a woman came looking for you after the fire. She said she was your mum's cousin."

Rae looked stunned.

"We may not be able to find her," Tara admitted, "but the library's a good place to start."

"I'm worried about the birds." Twitch nodded to the two bin bags in the corner. "They're precious. They need to be taken care of. After I've told mum that I'm camping out and got my stuff, I'm going to go to the shop and buy stuff to package them up properly and protect them."

"I don't want to ruin the vibe," Pam said. "But am I the only one who's going to mention the elephant in the room?"

They fell silent. Ava looked at Pam.

"The police are looking for Rae—" Pam said.

"We're not going to the police." Ava cut her off.

"Yes, Ava, I heard you the first time." Pam rolled her eyes. "I hadn't finished. Don't you think there might be *other* people looking for her?"

"Yes," Jack agreed. "I've been thinking about that too."

"What?" Tippi asked.

"Rae knows everything about the Dead Zoo Gang's

crimes," Jack said. "If I were them, I'd want her silenced. If the police find her, they will all end up in jail."

"They'll never find us here," Terry said.

There was an uncomfortable silence.

"Maybe we should go to the police," Tara suggested, looking nervous.

"But then Rae will go to jail," Tippi said.

"I'm not going to the police," Rae said. "They'll take Caliban away."

"I had a different idea," Pam said. "I was thinking that we could do with some extra muscle."

"Hey!" Terry held up his stick-thin arm and flexed it, popping up a gobstopper of a bicep. "What are you saying?"

"Permission to ask Vernon if he will help us?" Pam looked around.

"Let's vote," Jack said. "Hands up if you're in favour of bringing Vernon in."

Everyone except Rae put up their hand.

"All right, Pam, invite Vernon." Jack nodded.

"Vernon is the biggest kid we know," Ava explained to Rae. "He's good to have on your side in a fight."

After the meeting, the mood shifted to one of industry as they all set about their tasks. Tara ventured off to get permission from her mum for the girls to camp out before heading to the library. Twitch raced off on his bike, and had barely been gone half an hour before he was back with his camping gear and bird skin wrapping equipment.

Ava and Tippi stayed at the hide with Rae, while Jack cycled home to make an anonymous call to the police about Arch 645. He returned with a loaded rucksack.

It felt good to be doing something and, as they set up camp, Ava could feel her spirits lifting. She helped Twitch take each stolen bird skin, gently wrapping it in a paper towel, then placing it into a ziplock bag and sealing it. Twitch had emptied a plastic storage box that they used for birdwatching books, and he reverently placed the sealed bird skins inside.

Terry and Ozuru arrived pushing wheelbarrows filled with sleeping bags, roll mats, lanterns and other camping gear.

"Wow!" a low voice said from beyond the hide. "Did you guys build all of this yourselves?"

"Yes," Pam replied, as she brought Vernon into camp.

"All right, Vernon," Jack called out.

"Pammy says we're all camping out here tonight." Vernon grinned. "I love camping."

"There's not enough space in the hide for all of us,"

Ozuru said, "so I brought a four-man tent and extra air beds."

"Tonight, Vernon," Twitch said, "your job is to guard Rae."

"Who's Rae?" Vernon looked around.

"I am," Rae said, from her log by the fire. "But I don't need a bodyguard."

"You sure?" Vernon asked her. "Because I've always wanted to be one."

"Go on, Rae," Pam said. "Let him. It'll make him so happy."

Rae looked at Vernon, then nodded.

"Brilliant!" Vernon clapped his massive hands together. "Right, where are we going to pitch this tent?"

Vernon's arrival made Ava think of Jasper, Phil and Baz. She wondered what Jasper had done when he woke up in Arch 645 and found Rae gone.

Tara was the last to return. She waved Rae and Ava into the triangle room.

"Did you find anything?" Ava asked her as they sat down.

"I think so." Tara looked at Rae. "The newspapers said your mum's maiden name was Harriet Morton."

"Yes… I think that's right," Rae stammered. "I don't remember."

"I tracked down your parents' obituaries in the *Swanhurst Gazette*." She grimaced apologetically. "There was a sentence saying someone called Thea Morton attended their funeral. In the births, marriages and deaths register, I found a Morton family in a town called Beakhampton, about an hour from Swanhurst. They had a daughter called Harriet, who married a Walter Rackem."

"My parents," Rae said.

"Yes." Tara went on. "In Beakhampton, there is a woman called Thea Morton. I found her online; she's a schoolteacher. She's the right age to be your mum's cousin."

"Thea Morton," Rae repeated.

"I messaged her," Tara said. "I told her I knew where you were, that you were in trouble and needed the help of family."

"Do you think she'll reply?" Rae bit her lip nervously. "She might not want anything to do with me. She might call the police!"

"Best not to think about it." Tara patted her arm. "It might not even be the right person."

"Well done, Tara," Ava said. "Good detective work."

"Yes," Rae said. "Thank you."

"Why is Twitch playing with the dead birds?" Pam said, staring into the cabin. "That boy is so weird."

251

Tara, Ava and Rae glared at her.

"Weird—ly lovely," Pam added hastily. "He's weird *and* lovely, which really is the best combination."

Twitch was showing the last unwrapped bird skins to Tippi.

"... this is the resplendent quetzal. Look at the scarlet plumage on its breast."

"Shiny," Tippi marvelled.

"Check out this ribbon of tail feathers."

"What's this?" Tippi pointed at a small crimson bird with a white breast.

"King bird-of-paradise." Twitch carefully put down the resplendent quetzal and picked it up. "Also called the 'living gem'. Did you know, birds of paradise are related to corvids?"

Rae leaned forward and Ava saw that Vernon had come to the entrance of the hide and was also listening to Twitch.

"Crows and ravens?" Tippi looked at the colourful bird with astonishment.

"Yes. Some of them have similar skills. They mimic sounds, for example, but they're most famous for their beauty and their dancing."

"I'd like to see them dancing," Tippi said.

"Me too," Twitch agreed wistfully.

Jack came into the hide, budging Ava up so he could squeeze into the triangle room.

"Rae." Jack's intense tone immediately drew Ava's attention. "This is going to sound like an odd question, but how many sugars does your uncle Tony take in his coffee?"

"Three," Rae replied.

"Also, I wanted to ask you if you remember anything about the night your house burned down?"

Rae shook her head. "I remember going to sleep in the shed with Caliban. The next thing I remember was waking up in the hospital."

"You don't remember anything at all?" Ava asked.

"No."

Jack thought about this for a moment. "And, when your uncle collapsed, you didn't notice anything suspicious about it?"

"No one was near him," Rae said. "Caliban was throwing sugar cubes at Jasper, and making his alarm call..."

"...and Jasper tried to shut him up, by swinging for him with the elephant tusk?" Jack asked.

"Yes, but, Jack, I don't think Uncle Tony was murdered. Everyone in that arch was family and the only person with a motive" – Rae blinked – "is me."

"This is the flame bowerbird." Twitch picked up

a blazing yellow and red bundle of feathers. "It's one of the world's most brightly coloured birds and it does the freakiest dance. The MacGregor's bowerbird builds tall towers that can take years. The male bird does impersonations to impress a female, but the funniest bit is the peekaboo dance."

"Peekaboo dance?"

"The bird does his mimicking from behind his bower tower to get the female's attention. When she peeps round to see him, he hops out of sight." Twitch hopped around the edge of the table to demonstrate. Tippi hopped towards him, he hopped away again, and they both laughed.

Everyone was watching, even Pam.

Once the birds were safely packed away, and Ozuru's tent was up, Vernon and Jack set off to gather wood for the fire. Before long they were dining on veggie sausage sandwiches and baked beans.

"I was thinking," Twitch said as they sat around the fire, "of taking a taxi to the Swan Museum early tomorrow morning and leaving the bird skins on the doorstep, addressed to Dr Nutt." He had noted down the exact number and species of each bird as he'd packed them into the two storage boxes. All the birds were fully intact with their data tags.

"That would be one problem off our list," Jack agreed.

"Brrrrr. It's getting really cold." Tara clasped her coat hood around her neck.

A white flake wafted past Ava's face, vanishing as it neared the fire. "Was that snow?"

Everyone looked up. A low full moon illuminated the whirl of white specks swirling above their heads.

"It's snowing!" Tippi cried with delight, sticking her tongue out to catch a flake.

"It won't settle," Terry said. "It's not heavy enough."

"We should go inside," Jack said. "Cold I can handle. Wet and cold is unbearable."

Everyone got up slowly, reluctant to leave the warmth of the fire but not wanting to sit in the snow.

Rae and Tippi crawled into the triangle room.

"I'll be in in a minute," Ava called after them. "I want to have a quick word with Jack."

Jack was still standing beside the fire. He was staring into the trees. Ava turned to see what he was looking at and froze. In the darkness, beyond the footpath, she glimpsed a torch beam. Her heart stopped. Yes. There it was. A moving light.

"Quick. Put out the fire!" she called to Ozuru in a hushed voice. "There's someone out there!"

27
BARN OWL SPLITS

"Could you see who it was?" Jack whispered, as Ava and Terry quickly turned off the lanterns. Tara and Ozuru each grabbed a bucket of earth from beside the fire pit and dumped it on the flames. Ozuru took Tara's empty bucket and ran to the edge of the pond, stamping on it to break the surface ice, filling the buckets, and hurrying back to pour the water over the smoking heap of earth. There was a low sizzling sound as the fire went out.

Twitch had shinned up the ladder to the viewing platform above the hide and, in the light of the full moon, Ava could see him with binoculars pressed to his eyes. Jack lifted his binoculars. Twitch was signing a message. Ava could barely see the pale blur of Twitch's hands moving.

"Three men. On the main path," Jack whispered as he read. "Dead Zoo Gang!"

"What?" Ava felt her stomach clench with fear. "How did they find us? Twitch got rid of Caliban's tracker. How can they know where to look for Rae?"

"I don't know," Jack whispered, as Twitch shinned down the ladder and came running towards them.

"Huddle up," Twitch whispered, as Tippi and Rae were ushered out of the hide by Vernon.

"We need to hide in the hide," Terry said, looking panicked.

"If we're together we can be easily trapped," Jack said.

"There are three of them and ten of us," Twitch said calmly as they formed a tight circle. "One on one, they're stronger than us, but together, we're stronger than them. We need to split them up. Each of them has a torch and is carrying something that looks like a watering can."

"A watering can?" Tara frowned.

"Petrol," Rae said with chilling certainty.

"What are they planning to do?" Jack looked appalled. "Burn the woods down?"

"Flush me out." Rae nodded.

There was a horrible silence.

"Listen, you didn't ask to get mixed up in my mess. They're my family," Rae said. "You don't have to stay with me."

"You took our oath," Twitch told her. "You're a Twitcher now. We're all in this together."

"But they don't know that!" Ava said, feeling a surge of confidence. "They think Rae's alone. They don't know about us. Well, not *all* of us. We've got the element of surprise on our side."

"We can't take down all three of them at once," Jack said.

"I could try," Vernon volunteered.

"I've got an idea," Jack said. "Vernon, you and Tippi stay here in the hide with Rae. If anyone tries to grab her, smash them into smithereens."

"Got it." Vernon grinned.

"We need to get rid of those petrol cans," Twitch said. "Fire in a forest is a disaster, even in winter."

"We'll divide into teams," Jack said. "Ava, Tara and Pam, do you think you can handle Baz?" Ava nodded. "Terry and Ozuru, you take Phil Rackem. Twitch and I will take Jasper. Our objective is to separate them, take out the petrol cans, confuse them, make them think they're lost."

"We'll split up and approach the men from three different directions," Twitch said. "Whatever happens, don't let them set fire to the woods. The damage to the wildlife would be catastrophic."

"This is not my idea of fun," Pam said, looking nervous.

"You're going to get the best news story of your career tonight," Jack said encouragingly. "Make the most of it."

"We need to call the police," Tara said to Rae.

"But there's no mobile signal in the woods," Ava reminded her.

The high-pitched shriek of a barn owl on the wing made everyone jump.

"What was that?" Pam grabbed Tara, looking terrified.

"Just a barn owl," Ava replied, and an image popped into her head. "Hey, that's just given me an idea of a way to trap Uncle Baz."

"How?" Tara asked.

"Quick. Into the hide. Each of you is going to need a rope. We'll get them from the cabin."

"Don't you need a rope?" Pam asked as the three of them hurried inside.

"No, but I do need you to swap jumpers with me." Ava unzipped her coat and pulled off her black hoodie. Her top knot came undone and her hair fell around her shoulders. Pam took off her pink fluffy jumper with the white kitten on it and handed it over.

"Why do you need it?" she asked.

"Because I'm going to be the bait for our Baz trap."
Ava grinned. She'd been frightened of the Dead Zoo
Gang in the railway arch, but this was Aves Wood: this
was her turf and she knew every twist and turn of it.
"I'll tell you what we're going to do on the way there."

Armed with a couple of ropes, the three girls crept
into the trees, keeping a safe distance from the main
footpath, where Baz, Phil and Jasper were searching
for Rae. They looped round to a clearing north of the
path and in front of the men. Moonlight illuminated
the forest floor as Ava and Tara quickly tied a noose at
the end of each rope, pulling it into a wide circle about
a metre in diameter. They lay the nooses on the ground,
checking the distance between them, then covered the
ropes with leaf mulch and brown bracken.

"Pam, this is your tree," Ava said, trailing the rope
to the tree and wrapping it around the trunk, handing
the end to Pam. "You're going to hide behind it. And
whatever happens, don't show yourself." She pointed to
a tree opposite. Tara was wrapping her rope around it.
"Tara's going to hide there."

She went and stood in the clearing between the two
noose traps. "When I give the signal, you pull your rope
as hard as you can. Got that?"

Tara and Pam both gave her a thumbs up.

Ava collected a handful of small stones and put them in her pocket. Crouching down close to the path, she waited. The tiny flakes of snow that had been twirling about in the air had become fatter, fluffier ones.

Before long, Ava heard footsteps approaching.

"Can you smell something?" Phil asked.

"Smell what?" Baz replied.

"Campfire."

"If you'd let me burn the woods down," came Jasper's snide voice, "we'd soon flush the girl out."

"And what if she isn't here?" Baz growled. "We're in enough trouble without adding arson to the list."

"If you're not going to let Jasper burn the woods, why did we bring petrol?" Phil asked.

"Because, if we find that wretched girl and her dumb bird," Baz said, "she can't be allowed to live. Not after what she did to Tony. And a fire in a wood is a good way of making murder look like a tragic accident. Especially if Jasper is right and she's camping out here somewhere."

"She's a danger to us," Jasper said. "If the police find her before we do, she could put all three of us in prison for life."

The three men came into view, moving at a snail's pace, peering into the trees either side of the path.

Phil was hanging back and sniffing the air. He looked in the direction of the hide. "The campfire smell is coming from that way." He took two steps off the path, heading towards the pond. "I'm going to check it out."

"You're certain she's in this wood?" Baz asked Jasper.

"Oh, she's here all right," Jasper said. "She's got three little friends, and they told her to come here."

To Ava's horror, Jasper pulled a piece of paper from his pocket with her handwriting on it. It was the note she'd given to Rae. It was her fault that the Dead Zoo Gang had found them!

"Tell you what, why don't we call this number – see if it rings?"

A moment too late, Ava realized that Jasper was dialling *her* number. She scrabbled at the zip of her coat pocket, fumbling to take out her phone before it gave away her location. Her shaking hands failed to get a grip on it. It slipped, landing on the ground with a thud.

Baz turned to look in her direction.

"What is wrong with this place?" Jasper cursed, lifting his phone. "There's no signal!"

Ava offered up a silent prayer of thanks to Aves Wood for not letting phones work amongst their tree trunks.

Baz took a step towards her hiding place, and Ava held her breath.

"Where's Phil gone?" Jasper turned. "Phil?"

This was her chance to separate Baz from the group. Taking a stone from her pocket, Ava threw it at a tree close to where the man was peering into the undergrowth. The noise made him start. He checked himself, taking first one step, then another, off the path.

Ava glanced at Jasper, but he was following his brother into the trees on the other side of the path.

Slipping behind the trunk of a broad oak, Ava took aim, and threw a second stone as hard and as far as she could past Baz.

The pug-faced man waded through the brambles and dead bracken towards the clearing and the trap.

Careful to be silent, Ava crept from tree trunk to tree trunk, opening her coat as she entered the clearing and stood between the two rope nooses.

Baz had his back to her, shining his torch at the undergrowth where her stone had landed. Taking a deep breath, Ava aimed a stone at the man's back. It found its mark.

"Huh!" Baz spun around, waving his torch. He spotted Ava in Pam's bright pink jumper and looked startled.

Ava blew a raspberry at him.

Suddenly he was running towards her.

Every muscle in Ava's body screamed at her to run, but she needed to hold her nerve for the trap to work. She held her arms above her head as if surrendering and when Baz was two metres from her, she threw herself into a backflip, kicking the torch out of his hands. It arced high and was swallowed by the undergrowth.

Ava's eyes had adjusted to the moonlit woods, but Baz was momentarily blind.

"Why, you little…"

Ava dropped into a crouch, watching as Baz cautiously stepped one foot forward.

"Where are you, little girl?" Baz muttered menacingly, taking a second step forward. "I know you're here."

Ava stared at the noose, willing his left foot to move forward just one more step.

"Is Rae with you?" Baz said. "We've got a present for her."

Suddenly Ava launched herself up, screeching like a barn owl.

Shocked, Baz stumbled, stepping his left foot in Pam's noose. His right foot was close to the edge of Tara's but not inside. Ava lurched forwards, kicking at his ankle. His right foot bounced into Tara's noose.

"NOW!" she yelled.

Pam and Tara tugged hard on their ropes. The nooses snapped shut around Baz's ankles and his feet flew out in opposite directions.

A high-pitched, unearthly *"Yowl!"* echoed through the trees as Baz landed in the splits, falling face first in the snow-speckled dirt.

Darting in, Ava grabbed the can of petrol that he'd dropped, while Tara and Pam speedily secured their ropes tight around the tree trunks. Then all three of them ran.

28

SHAKE YOUR
TAIL FEATHER

Ava, Tara and Pam sprinted to the kissing gate that opened onto the canal towpath. As they came through, they finally dared to look back. No one seemed to be following them.

"One down," Ava said, breathless and exhilarated.

"Two to go," Tara finished. "Phil was heading towards the hide."

"Jasper's the one I'm worried about: he's dangerous," Ava said. "Here, have you got a bit of spare rope?"

Tara handed her a small roll from her pocket. "What are you doing?"

"Making sure this can of petrol is out of play." Ava checked the lid was screwed on tight, then tied the rope to the handle and lowered it into the canal. "We'll fish it out later" – she fastened the end of the rope to a mooring ring – "when no one is trying to burn anything."

"Did you hear the noise that gangster made when he did the splits?" Pam giggled.

"Serves him right," Tara said. "He came here to capture Rae. He deserves worse." She touched Ava's arm. "Look, I know you made Rae a promise, but they're here to kill her. I want to call the police. Crowther Bridge is right there." She looked up the canal. "I can get a signal on it."

"I agree," Pam said.

Ava knew Tara was right. Tippi was with Rae in the hide, which was where Phil and Jasper were heading. She nodded. They needed help.

"Meet you back at the hide," Ava called out as Tara ran up the towpath.

Jogging through the woods, scanning ahead for enemies, Ava led Pam back. The snow was coming down heavily now.

As they moved through the woods, Ava thought about the Rackems. Baz wasn't a natural leader. Phil didn't seem very bright. Jasper was the dangerous one. With Tony gone, Jasper would surely become the leader of the Dead Zoo Gang. He'd finally get to pull off the big bank jobs he'd talked to Phil about that morning.

The girls kept to the edge of the boggy land around the pond as they approached the hide. The moon was reflected in the freezing water, and as the hide came into view, the sight that greeted them was a strange one.

Ava saw Tippi – dressed in brightly coloured clothes – and Vernon creeping around the outside of the hide.

"Why is your sister wearing my banana hoodie as a pair of trousers?" Pam exclaimed in a cross whisper. "She's getting it dirty!"

Ava watched as Tippi peeped around the hide, let out a scream, then raced back to stand behind Vernon. Phil Rackem appeared, thundering after her, but as soon as he turned the corner, Vernon, who was ready and waiting, punched him hard on the nose. Phil roared, his hands flying to his face as he bent forward in pain. Vernon and Tippi immediately disappeared around the hide. A second later, Ava saw Tippi's head peeping out the other side. Her little sister waited until Phil had straightened up. She let out a scream and disappeared again. Growling, Phil pivoted and dashed after her. Ava heard another roar of pain. A second later Tippi and Vernon came racing into view, a look of glee on their faces. Once again, Tippi peeped and screamed, but this time she grabbed Vernon and pointed for him to face the other direction.

Attempting to outwit Tippi, Phil came blundering around the opposite side of the hide, but Vernon was waiting – he punched Phil hard on the nose again. Taken by surprise, Phil fell backwards, hitting the ground hard and letting go of his petrol can. As he rolled around on the floor, clutching his nose, Tippi delivered a swift, hard kick to the man's side before grabbing the can and running away.

"What are they doing?" Pam said, sounding baffled.

"I think" – Ava felt a burst of pride at her sister's cleverness and bravery – "Tippi is being a bowerbird!"

"Oh no!" Pam gasped as Jasper stalked into the clearing.

"What is wrong with you?" Jasper looked at his brother with disgust. "Why are you rolling around on the ground?"

"I … uh…" Phil sat up. Blood was streaming from his nose, and he didn't seem to be able to open his eyes. "There's a little girl in the woods who punches like a heavyweight boxer! She stole my petrol."

"Don't be ridiculous." Jasper looked around, pointing his torch into the trees, shaking his head. "Why do I always have to do everything myself?"

Ava found she was holding her breath. He hadn't seen the hide yet, but he would, any second. "We've got to do something," she whispered.

"Rae's here, I know she is," Jasper said, and then his torch stopped on the cabin. "Aha!"

There was a movement in the doorway of the hide. Suddenly Rae bolted out of it, sprinting into the trees. Jasper crowed with delight and raced after her.

"She has no idea where she's going!" Ava looked at Pam in alarm.

As Phil climbed to his feet a net descended over his head and torso. A second later, Terry and Ozuru were encircling him with a length of rope. Phil tried to shrug them off, but Tippi appeared in front of him, drawing back her fist as if to punch him. He looked at her in horror as Vernon appeared behind him and kicked at the backs of his knees, knocking him to the ground. Phil wriggled like a giant worm as Terry and Ozuru bound him tightly, securing his hands and feet.

"Ava." Tara came racing up behind her. "Rae needs our help."

With a jolt, Ava turned. "Which way did she go?"

"This way." Throwing caution to the wind, Tara ran out into the open.

Ava sprinted after her. Snow was falling heavily

now. Flakes stuck to Ava's hair. She inhaled them as she ran. Two of the Dead Zoo Gang were out of action. There was just Jasper left. Where were Jack and Twitch? They were supposed to have stopped Jasper. An icy fear stole through Ava's blood as she glanced about for her friends. She hoped they were all right.

Tara's arm flew out, halting her. She dropped to the ground, so Ava did too, followed by Pam who was trying to catch her breath.

"*Over there,*" Tara signed and pointed.

A hundred metres through the trees, Ava saw Rae backing away from Jasper. She looked frightened. His torch was pointed at her face.

"You stupid little witch!" Jasper snarled. "Your spell over us died with Dad. Your pathetic pity act doesn't work on me. You're the only weak chink in my armour and I'm about to fix you." He put the torch down on the ground, angled up at her.

Rae shuffled back until her spine hit the trunk of a tree. There was nowhere for her to go. Ava felt frozen to the spot. She didn't know what to do.

"I'm going to enjoy this," Jasper laughed, unscrewing the cap of his petrol can.

"I didn't kill Uncle Tony," Rae blurted out.

"Poor stupid little Rae." Jasper's laugh was high and

wild like a hyena's call. "It was you who tipped off the police about the arch, wasn't it?" He leered at her. "I always knew you were a *traitor*. Well, you might like to know that the arch was empty by the time they arrived. Your little plan didn't work. But I've carefully selected some of our loot and stashed it in your old shed, for the police to find." Rae pressed her lips together, saying nothing. "You don't need to worry about going to prison, though, because you'll be dead soon." He laughed in her face. "I'm the head of the Dead Zoo Gang now."

He held up the petrol can, jerking it towards Rae, who flinched.

Ava expected to see an arc of gasoline but as the can rose, Jack darted out from behind the tree with a long stick. He whacked the bottom of it, so that it flew up, spinning and spraying petrol all over Jasper's trousers.

The leader of the Dead Zoo Gang howled with rage.

"Yes, Jack!" Ava whispered, punching the air.

Jack sprinted away and Jasper made to chase after him, but then he stopped and turned around, looking back at Rae and shaking his head. "I'm not falling for your tricks." His mouth split into a razor-blade smile. "I'll take care of your friends after I've finished with you." He picked up the canister of petrol. This time he didn't fling it at Rae. He walked straight up to her and poured it over her head.

"What do we do?" Pam asked, horrified.

But Ava and Tara were already sprinting through the trees towards Rae. Tara was removing her coat as she ran. Ava saw Jack and Twitch hurtling towards Rae from the opposite direction.

Jasper had a chunky silver lighter in his hand. He sparked it. "Say hello to Mummy and Daddy."

Everything seemed to slow down.

Jasper threw the lighter at Rae and stepped back. As the flame spun in the air, a dark shadow dropped from the tree above. Claws grabbed the silver body of the lighter, catching it before it met its target. With three flaps of his wings, Caliban was over Jasper's head. Jasper threw up his hands, stumbling backwards. His foot hit a tree root and he fell to the ground. The raven dropped the lighter and there was a *whoooomph!* noise as Jasper's trousers went up in flames.

"*Argh!*" Jasper screamed, rolling over and kicking his legs, trying to put out the fire.

"Caliban!" Rae cried out, looking up at her bonded bird. She didn't see the trail of fire shooting towards her, tracing the line of petrol across the forest floor.

"Rae!" Ava screamed, but Tara was ahead of her. She

threw herself at the girl, knocking her off her feet and away from the tree. The flames raced after them. Ava jumped on them, stamping her feet madly. Tara used her coat like a blanket, flattening the flames. A second later, Jack and Twitch were beside Ava, putting out the fire.

The wailing Jasper had kicked off his shoes, undone his petrol-soaked jeans and was peeling them off whilst writhing about on the forest floor. He managed to put out the flaming trousers only for the arm of his jacket to catch alight! He got to his feet and ran, howling, through the trees, in his pants, to the bank of the pond, where he hurled himself into the icy water.

29
FLYING ACCUSATIONS

Rae wriggled out from under Tara. "Caliban!" she called, and a shadow descended. The raven perched on Rae's knees. She bowed her head to him. He rubbed his feathered crown against her cheek.

"Boop boop," Rae said softly.

"Boop boop," Caliban replied.

In the distance, Ava became aware of sirens. She heard running feet and got up, standing defensively before Rae. A light was beamed into her face, blinding her, and she staggered back, her arm shielding her eyes. She felt Tara and Jack either side of her.

"This is the police. Stay right where you are," came a voice through a loudhailer. "We have you surrounded."

There was the thudding of more feet. More lights switched on, illuminating the wild swirling snow.

Terry and Ozuru came to stand beside Twitch, and

275

Vernon and Tippi stood beside Tara, completing the protective circle around Rae and Caliban.

"Where's Pam?" Tara asked, but Ava couldn't see her.

"She was with us a moment ago," Ava replied.

"Arrest them!" Jasper shrieked, emerging from the pond. His coat was singed and dripping wet. His thin naked legs were lilac-blue and he was shivering. "Arrest them n-n-now!" He waved his finger at them. "They s-s-set fire to m-m-me."

"Did not!" Jack shouted back. "You did that to yourself with *your* petrol and *your* lighter."

Jasper's whole body was shuddering. An officer ran forward with a foil blanket. Jasper snatched it and wrapped it around his waist like a skirt. "That girl." He pointed at Rae. "She's a thief. She stole the birds from the Swan Museum! These children are all criminals! They probably have the birds in their secret lair back there."

Ava's stomach tightened. Jasper was twisting everything to make them look like the bad guys!

"We do have the bird skins," Twitch called out in a clear, calm voice. "They're stored safely in watertight containers. I've made an itemized list of all the species. You can let Dr Nutt know that they still have their tags. We were going to return them to the museum tomorrow morning."

"HA! They admit it!" Jasper cackled. "Arrest them. They've confessed."

Rae tapped Ava on the shoulder. She and Tara moved to make room for her to stand between them. The stink of petrol from her clothes was alarming. Ava took a sideways look at the girl with her raven.

"I remember," she said to Jasper in a small, brave voice. "When you were standing in front of me just now, in the darkness, holding your petrol can, I remembered!"

Jasper went rigid; his mouth clamped shut.

"I remembered another night," Rae said, her voice growing in strength. "Two years ago, in the darkness, I remember you with another petrol can, when you started the fire that burned down my home and killed my parents. *I remember. You were there!*" Rae was shaking with anger. "*I saw you!*"

Ava felt the power in Rae's words and knew they were the truth. Every cell in her body was aflame with sorrow and rage for her friend's loss. Tears filled her eyes.

"That girl is a murderer!" Jasper screamed, pointing at Rae again. "She killed my father. I demand justice!"

Ava clenched her fists with anger, feeling her nails cutting into her palms.

"You are *all* under arrest!" boomed a man's voice through the loudhailer. "You do not have to say anything. But it may harm your defence if you do not mention when questioned something which you later rely on in court. Anything you do say may be given in evidence."

Ava gasped and felt Tippi take her hand.

"NO!" Jasper shouted. He faked a run at one of the officers, then turned and dashed away along the edge of the pond, his silver skirt flying out behind him. Five police officers raced after him.

"Oh dear," Twitch said quietly. "Don't go that way!"

There was a splash as Jasper disappeared up to his middle in icy bog water. Two police officers went down with him.

"Good evening," Jack said politely as four uniformed officers approached them. He looked up at the snow that was flurrying around them. "I think I speak on behalf of all of the Twitchers when I say we are very keen to get to the warm police station and help you with your enquiries."

"I d-d-definitely am," Terry said through chattering teeth, offering up his wrists.

"We're not going to handcuff you." The officer sounded mildly amused.

"Junior Police Cadet Vernon Boon," Vernon said, saluting her, "at your service, ma'am."

The silhouette of an approaching man, backlit by floodlights, became the familiar figure of Constable Greenwood. Ava's relief to see him wasn't marred by the stern expression on his face. "What on earth have you lot got yourself mixed up in?" he muttered, looking unhappy.

"Nice to see you too, Constable Greenwood," Jack said, cheerily.

"This is serious, Jack." Constable Greenwood shook his head. "I'm going to have to call all of your parents when we get back to the station." He took a moment to look at each of them. "You are all in a lot of trouble."

Ava's heart sank. Her mum was never going to forgive her. It was a long drive to Briddvale. She'd be grounded for ever and never allowed to visit her friends again. Tippi shuffled up against her side and Ava felt the whole group drawing closer together.

"We know it's serious, Constable," Tara replied, sweetly. "That man" – she pointed at Jasper who was being hauled out of the water and handcuffed – "and two others came into Aves Wood to try and kill our friend. That's why I called you. We were camping out in the hopes of seeing a snow goose."

"Two others?" Constable Greenwood frowned.

"Constable Greenwood," an officer said, approaching

him. "We've found a man in a clearing by the footpath suspended between two trees. He says his name is Baz Rackem. Shall we read him his rights and cuff him?"

Constable Greenwood turned to look at the Twitchers. "Suspended between two trees?"

"On the ground," Tara explained, an innocent expression on her face.

"Th-there's another one t-t-tied up by the pond," Terry admitted.

"His name is Phil Rackem," Tippi said helpfully.

"That one's Jasper Rackem." Jack pointed at the struggling man in socks and underpants being dragged away by two police officers. "They are the Dead Zoo Gang."

30

THE CROAKING RAVEN

Constable Greenwood escorted the children through the east gate and into the car park.

"Are you all right?" Ava fell into step beside Rae. Caliban was perched protectively on her shoulder, threading his beak through her hair.

"I think so. I don't know," Rae replied, giving her a weak smile. "Bit scared."

"Me too," Ava admitted, "but it's going to be OK. Constable Greenwood is a good guy and we're all together."

A police officer approached them carrying an animal cage. "I'm afraid I'm going to need you to put your bird into the cage, just while we're in the van and at the station. But you can carry the cage, if you want."

"OK." Rae opened the cage door, putting her hand inside. "In, Caliban. In." The raven hopped along her arm, obediently going into the cage. Rae put her forehead to the bars and said softly, "Boop boop."

"Boop boop," Caliban replied.

There were three police vans in the car park. The Twitchers were clambering into the back of one, when Ava heard Pam calling out, "Wait for me!" Pam sprinted into the car park with her camera in her hand, scrambling into the van and sitting on the bench beside Ava. "Budge up."

"Have you been filming this whole time?" Ava asked.

"Of course!" Pam replied in an excited whisper. "I got Jasper Rackem on fire and everything!"

As the doors of the van were being closed, they saw a limping Baz Rackem, with his hands cuffed behind his back, and a swollen-eyed Phil Rackem being escorted through the trees by officers.

Constable Greenwood got into the passenger seat in the front of the van, nodding to the officer behind the wheel. There was a rectangular mesh window in a metal barrier between him in the front and them in the back. He slid it open, so they could see his face clearly.

"Are you all right?" He looked at them with concern, but they all nodded. "There are blankets under the seat if you're cold."

Terry immediately bent down and grabbed a bundle.

"Constable Greenwood." There was urgency in Jack's voice. "You need to know. Jasper Rackem is a killer. He murdered Rae's parents and I believe he may have killed his own dad."

"Woah." Constable Greenwood held up a hand. "Firstly" – he pointed up to a small CCTV camera – "anything you say in here is being recorded. Do you all understand that?" Ten heads nodded. "Right, now, back up a bit. Start from the beginning."

Jack looked at Ava. She told Constable Greenwood about being at the Swan Museum when the robbery happened and that they'd been investigating the theft. When she got to the part where she, Jack and Twitch had set out that morning to rescue Rae, Jack interrupted.

"Constable Greenwood, we were there when Antony Rackem was carried out to the van and taken to the hospital. Rae said he'd had a heart attack."

"That's what it looked like." Rae nodded.

"We only learned he had died from the radio," Jack said, "which reported that his death was being treated as suspicious."

"That's correct," Constable Greenwood confirmed.

"Why is it suspicious?"

"Because Antony Rackem didn't die of a heart attack."

"He was poisoned then," Jack said. "Wasn't he?"

Constable Greenwood's eyebrows lifted. "I couldn't possibly comment."

"What do you mean, poisoned?" Rae asked.

"Rae." Jack turned to her. "I think that the night your house was burned down, Caliban saw Jasper do it. Ravens remember human faces. He has always known what kind of a human Jasper is."

"That's why he's always hated him!" Rae said in wonder.

"I think your uncle came to your house that night, to try and stop Jasper, but he was too late. I think he called out Jasper's name, knowing what he'd done, and that's the cry that Caliban mimics. *Jasper! No! Jasper! No!* Jasper knows it too."

"But what's that got to do with Uncle Tony being poisoned?" Rae asked.

"When Twitch and I were hiding outside the arch, and Ava was with you in the cage, Jasper went over to the sugar bowl and coated the sugar lumps with poison. You told me that your uncle likes three sugars in his coffee."

"Yes."

"Jasper then went to the cafe with Phil to buy coffee." He looked at Constable Greenwood. "I'll bet you anything that, when you interview Phil about this, he'll tell you that Jasper forgot Uncle Tony's sugar. He had to use the sugar in the bowl."

"Oh!" Rae exclaimed, suddenly seeing what Jack was getting at.

"When your uncle added sugar to his coffee from that bowl, he was adding poison. The only one who saw Jasper coat the sugar was Caliban. He tried to warn your uncle with an alarm call, then he used your uncle's voice from the night of the fire to shout Jasper's name and threw sugar lumps at Jasper. That's why Jasper grabbed the elephant tusk and tried to shut him up. Caliban tried to save your uncle, but it was too late."

"The bird?" Constable Greenwood said, sounding sceptical.

"Caliban is incredibly clever," Twitch explained. "Most ravens are, but he is the smartest bird I've ever met."

"We've got evidence to corroborate our story," Ava said. "Jack filmed everything with his GoPro. I'm sure if you look back at the footage, you'll see sugar lumps all over the floor when we rescued Rae from Jasper."

"Yes," Jack said. "I know the arch was empty when the police searched it, but I filmed hundreds of stolen things, including the tusk that had been hacked off an elephant belonging to Louis XIV that, according to the label, belongs to the Paris Natural History Museum. It was the weapon Jasper used to give Rae that bump on her head."

"You got it all on film?" Constable Greenwood sounded amazed.

"Yes!" Pam said, swiping her hand through the air. "We filmed all of it."

"Constable Greenwood," Tara said. "What will happen when we get to the police station?" Ava heard the worry in her voice.

"I will eventually be sending all of you home tonight to sleep in a warm bed," Constable Greenwood said, "but we need to take statements first and your parents need to be here for that."

"What about Rae and Caliban?" Ava asked, seeing the frightened look on Rae's face.

"We've already put a call in to social services. Don't worry, Rae will be looked after."

"But she's got to stay with me," Twitch insisted. "Social services might be able to take care of Rae, but what about Caliban? They shouldn't be separated; he's all the family she has. If they stay with me, Rae and Caliban can have my bedroom. I think that would be best, don't you?" He looked questioningly at Rae, and she nodded. "I'll sleep on the sofa. My mum won't mind. She's used to me bringing home birds. She'll be surprised when she finds out there's a human attached to this one."

"I'll see what I can do, Twitch, but I can't promise anything," Constable Greenwood said. "It will be up to social services."

"Will…" Rae swallowed; her eyes brimmed with tears. "Will you look after Caliban if I have to go to prison?" she asked Twitch in a raw whisper.

"Young lady." Constable Greenwood turned to look her in the eye. "You will *not* be going to prison. I can tell you that right now."

And suddenly Rae was sobbing.

"Oh!" Ava exclaimed. "Don't cry!"

"It's all going to be OK." Tippi hugged her.

"I know … it's just…" Rae hiccupped as she struggled to get the words out. "You're all so … nice!"

31
DEAD BEAT CLAN

"Ah, Miss Hardacre." Constable Greenwood lifted the camera from her hands as she got out of the back of the van. He gave her an apologetic smile. "I'm afraid I am going to have to confiscate all of your film footage. We need it as evidence."

"What?" Pam gasped, looking horrified. "Will I get it back?"

"It will be returned to you after any court case has taken place," Constable Greenwood explained.

As they filed into Briddvale Police Station, Ava saw a woman in a brightly patterned dress and green cardigan get up from a chair in the waiting room. She had short, neat grey hair, glasses, and a reassuring air. She introduced herself to Constable Greenwood as Marilyn Evans from social services. Ava took Rae's free hand; the other one was clutching the handle of Caliban's cage.

"Nerissa," Constable Greenwood called to the desk officer. "Would you mind putting the children in the meeting room? And see if we can rustle up some hot drinks for them. I need to have a quick word with Ms Evans." He went to the door. "Oh, and we need to call their parents, so if you could take the numbers and let me know when they arrive." He pushed it open and paused. "And get Chief Superintendent Stickler from Swanhurst on the phone, would you?" Then he and the woman from social services disappeared.

Keeping a tight hold of Rae's hand, Ava followed Nerissa into a room that looked a lot like a classroom, with tables and chairs. They all sat down, but no one spoke. Ava felt anxious and could see everyone else did too. A male officer came in with a tray of watery hot chocolates and they gratefully picked up the sugary drinks.

Twitch's mum was the first to arrive; he'd messaged her from the van. Twitch left the room to talk to her. Through the glass walls, Ava saw Iris Featherstone hug her son, and then listen as he explained the situation. Glancing at Rae, Ava saw that Rae was watching them intently. Iris was nodding. Constable Greenwood appeared with Marilyn Evans, then the three adults disappeared through a door together, and Twitch returned. He gave Rae a thumbs up and an encouraging smile.

A few minutes later, Constable Greenwood came into the room. He held up his hands for quiet. "There's a lot happening this evening. I need you to be patient and hold on to your questions. I'll give you answers as and when I get them, but" – a twinkle came into his eye – "I thought you might enjoy watching me reading the charges to our suspects." He directed them to follow him into a small room. One of the walls was a window into another room. In it sat Jasper Rackem, Phil Rackem and Baz Rackem. All three were handcuffed.

Rae gasped.

"It's all right; they can't see you," Constable Greenwood reassured her.

"It's a two-way mirror!" Terry exclaimed. "Awesome!"

"Strictly speaking, it's a one-way mirror," Constable Greenwood said. "You can see them, but they can't see you. They can't hear you either, but there's a speaker up there. You'll be able to hear them. Right, let's see how they respond to the charges I'm about to level against them." He left the room and closed the door.

Ava stared around her in amazement. She'd seen places like this on TV shows, but never in real life. Jack looked delighted.

"We are not saying a word until we've got a lawyer," Jasper declared as Constable Greenwood entered the interrogation room with Officer Nerissa.

"I'm sorry to have to detain you, gentlemen," he said, ignoring Jasper. "I'm Constable Greenwood. I have to notify you that the camera up there is recording." He sat down opposite the three men. "I wanted to make it clear to you why we're holding you, what the allegations are against you and why we will be interviewing you. This is a complicated matter. So, I thought a little chat might clarify things for all of us, don't you agree?"

The Rackems glared at the two police officers in silence.

"The first matter concerns the deaths of Walter and Harriet Rackem, who died in a house fire two years ago in Cygnet Close."

"What? We've been through this before," Baz said. "That was a terrible tragedy. I loved my brother, Walter." He paused and then mumbled, "I loved both of them."

Constable Greenwood was looking at Jasper.

"I told the police at the time," Jasper sneered at him. "I have an alibi for that night. I was with my father."

"We'll come to him in a moment." Constable Greenwood nodded.

"Two new witnesses have come forward placing you,

Jasper Rackem, at the scene of the fire in Cygnet Close," Constable Greenwood said. "You were seen with a can of petrol in your hand."

"Two witnesses?" Jasper looked alarmed.

Ava glanced at Jack who smiled back.

"Thought you were nowhere near Walter's place?" Baz said to Jasper, frowning. "Tony said it was a tragic accident."

"I wasn't!" Jasper snapped. "It was!"

"The second matter we are investigating is the death of Antony Rackem. While it may have looked like a heart attack, toxicology tests have come back showing cyanide poisoning as the cause of death. We think it may have been given to him on sugar."

"Cyanide!" Baz and Phil looked shocked. Jasper's expression was blank.

"We believe he was murdered." Constable Greenwood looked at each of them. "Do you know of any reason someone might have wanted to kill Antony Rackem?"

They shook their heads. Baz's eyes flicked to Jasper. Phil was frowning as if he was attempting to solve a complicated puzzle in his head.

"The third matter we are investigating concerns this evening, and why you took it upon yourselves to attack local children in Aves Wood." He paused, looking at them in case they wanted to comment. They remained sullenly silent. "Considering the fresh allegations that you were seen at the site of the fire in Cygnet Close," he said to Jasper, "it looks particularly bad that, this evening, you were chasing after young Rae Rackem carrying petrol."

"The petrol was for my car." Jasper stuck his chin out. "It ran out. We had to walk to buy some more."

"The fourth matter concerns a robbery at the Swan Museum last week. The children you attempted to attack claim you were behind it, that you forced young Rae to do it, and that you are in fact the notorious Dead Zoo Gang. They claim the reason you were in Aves Wood this evening was to silence them."

"What fanciful rot," Jasper said.

"Does the name Dead Zoo Gang mean anything to you?" Constable Greenwood asked.

"Never heard of it," Jasper said. "Sounds like the kind of rubbish children make up."

"I understand you've been read your rights, is that correct?"

They nodded.

"Good." Constable Greenwood got up. "I won't be interviewing you. That will be Chief Superintendent

Stickler from Swanhurst, when he arrives. In the meantime, we'd better see about getting you that lawyer, hadn't we?" He and the other officer left the room.

"Is that it?" Jack said, sounding disappointed.

The door opened and Constable Greenwood joined them.

"They didn't confess," Ava said, feeling frustrated.

"Be patient," Constable Greenwood said, coming to look through the glass.

The three men sat in silence for several long minutes, then Phil said, "Jasper, why did that copper say Dad was poisoned?"

"I don't know," Jasper snapped. "He's lying."

"You forgot Dad's sugar in the cafe."

"Exactly," Jasper nodded. "I didn't put the sugar in it."

"You *were* in Cygnet Close that night, weren't you," Baz said, his sad, round pug-like eyes turned to Jasper. "I think I've always known Tony was protecting you."

"Would you two shut up," Jasper snapped. "We're being filmed."

"But you never appreciated what he did for you." Baz's voice was trembling with emotion. "What kind of a monster kills their own father?"

Ava saw the horror in Phil's eyes as he realized what his brother had done.

Suddenly Baz was on his feet, throwing his handcuffed hands over Jasper's head and trying to strangle him. Phil roared with grief and threw the table across the floor. Constable Greenwood hit a button on the wall and officers burst into the room, separating the three men and leading them away.

There was a long silence as the Twitchers all looked at each other.

"That's the end of the Dead Zoo Gang," Jack said.

"You're safe now," Ava said to Rae.

"They're the Dead Beat Clan now," Terry quipped.

Ava felt Tippi's hand slip into hers and she smiled at her little sister. "It's all going to be OK," she said.

"Course it is," Tippi replied. "We're the Twitchers."

32
FLOCK TOGETHER

"I feel at home here," Rae admitted bashfully to Ava. She had stayed with Twitch for three nights. Twitch had given his bedroom over to Rae and Caliban. She'd had invitations from the other Twitchers, but this was where Caliban was happy. "I like sleeping in the bird box bed."

Ava thought she understood. Twitch's bed had a cabin over the mattress, with a round hole for a door, like a bird box. When you crawled inside, the walls were decorated with bird posters and fairy lights.

"It feels safe inside," Rae told Ava as they sat down at Twitch's kitchen table with the rest of the gang. "And the bedroom window is always open so that Caliban can come and go as he pleases. He's never had so much freedom. He loves it here."

"Frazzle is too stupid to realize that Caliban could kill him and eat him quick as *that*." Twitch snapped his fingers. "The silly pigeon keeps following the raven around and annoying him."

"Aren't you worried that that might actually happen?" Jack asked.

"Not really. Caliban does what Rae says, and she's constantly telling him to leave the pigeons alone. He seems to understand that the pigeons are my family, like he is Rae's."

"I reckon Caliban thinks he's human," Tara said.

"He does like to eat with us at the dinner table," Twitch told them enthusiastically.

Today was Ava and Tippi's last day in Briddvale. Ava was savouring every second. Their mum had been surprisingly understanding about being called to the police station. She'd been proud of her daughters for helping Rae and told them that they would discuss it at the end of the holiday, when they came home. It was frustrating to have to leave her friends again, not knowing when they'd next be able to visit. "I can't bear that we're going to have to go home tomorrow."

"I know." Tippi screwed up her face. "I don't want to leave yet. Vernon was going to teach me how to punch people on the nose."

"Ozuru, do you think your dad would mention to our mum that Briddvale needs a good massage therapist when she picks us up tomorrow?" Ava asked. "We keep pestering her about moving here, but she doesn't listen."

"Yes." Tippi nodded. "She'd listen to your dad."

"I'll ask him," Ozuru promised.

"We'll see you next week at the museum," Tara reminded her.

The Swan Museum had been delighted to get their bird skins back. The care with which Twitch had wrapped and catalogued each one had impressed Dr Trudy Nutt. Wanting to thank the Twitchers, she'd invited them all to spend an afternoon having a private tour of the collections, followed by cake and tea. Terry had grumbled that a cash prize would have been better, but Ava was looking forward to it.

Rae glanced nervously at the kitchen clock for the hundredth time.

No one was talking about it, but they were here to support Rae, because today she was meeting Thea Morton, her mother's cousin.

The woman had replied eagerly to Tara's email, wanting to set up a meeting with Rae as soon as possible, even mentioning that she'd like to offer her a home. Marilyn, the social worker, had stepped in, taking over the communication, explaining that Rae was being cared for but was exhausted and overwhelmed by recent events. It was decided that a few days' rest before such a big meeting would be a good idea, and Twitch's mum had been happy to have Rae staying with them for as long as was needed.

The doorbell rang and they all jumped. Rae nervously pulled at the black long-sleeved T-shirt with pink arms that Pam had given her. She was wearing a pair of Tara's jeans and Terry's sister's old trainers. Food and a couple of days' rest had put colour in her cheeks, but she still obviously needed looking after.

Iris came into the kitchen. Behind her were Marilyn and a woman with a long face that made Ava think of a horse. There were freckles on her nose. She had smile lines around her green eyes and looked a little nervous.

"Hello, everyone," Marilyn said. "I'd like you to meet Thea."

"Hi!" they all replied.

Thea looked taken aback to see so many children. Her eyes skimmed over their faces, settling on Rae's, and she smiled warmly.

"We were just going upstairs." Twitch stood up. "It's time to feed the pigeons."

The Twitchers trailed out of the room, but Ava hung back, wanting to take her cue from Rae.

"It's OK," Rae whispered to her with a timid nod.

As Ava approached the woman, she extended her hand. "Nice to meet you, Miss Morton. My name is Ava. I'm Rae's best friend."

"Lovely to meet you, Ava, and please, call me Thea."

Ava scanned her face for any hint of meanness, crossness or malice, but found none. As she left the room, she gave Rae a thumbs up.

Taking the stairs two at a time, Ava went into Twitch's bathroom and stepped out of the open window onto the flat roof, where the others were all sitting cross-legged in front of the pigeon coop. Twitch had his head inside and was cleaning out the water bowls and topping up their grain.

"People love bird videos." Pam had her camera out and was filming the pigeons. "I made a short one of Caliban talking; you know, saying his name and going 'boop boop'. It's had thousands of views already. I was thinking I might make more, whilst I'm waiting to get my Dead Zoo Gang footage back. Can your pigeons do any cool tricks?"

"You know what video we're all dying to see?" Tara said.

"Which one?"

"The one you used to blackmail Terry."

"Yes!" everyone chimed in. "Show us! What is it?"

"I made Terry a promise." Pam shook her head.

"Come on, Terry," Tippi pleaded. "Ava and I have to go home tomorrow. Please?"

"Trust me. Nobody wants to see that video." Terry had gone pink.

"We're all dying to know what it is," Jack admitted.

"Pleeeeeeeaaaaassse!" Tippi begged. "OK, you don't have to show us it, just tell us what it is."

"It's nothing," Terry said.

"If it was nothing, Pam wouldn't have been able to blackmail you," Ozuru pointed out.

"Fine." Terry tried to look nonchalant. "If you must know, it was a video of me doing a wee in the bushes."

Ava frowned and looked at Jack, who looked similarly puzzled.

"Pam, did you film Terry doing a wee?" Jack asked.

"That's weird," Tippi said, and Ava nodded.

"Terry…" Pam said in a warning voice. She didn't like the judgemental way they were all looking at her.

"Fine. I was doing something else while I was doing a wee," Terry admitted with a huff.

"What was it?" Tara asked.

"I was… I was … singing the wee-wee song."

"What?" Ava stared at Terry, who was beginning to squirm. "What is the wee-wee song?"

"Something my mum used to sing, when I was little."

"Oh, we've got to hear the wee-wee song." Jack was grinning.

"Come on, Terry," Ava cajoled. "Sing it for us."

"Yes! Please! Sing it!" they chorused.

"Sing it, sing it, sing it," Jack chanted.

"Fine, but only if you promise not to laugh," Terry said sullenly.

"We promise."

Looking resigned, Terry drew in a deep breath, and they all fell silent.

Then, to the tune of the Christmas carol "Hark the Herald Angels Sing", he sang:

"Do you want to be a big boy,

Do your wee-wees standing up?

Pants must be around your ankles

And the toilet seat pushed up.

Don't dance around or get distracted,

You'll make a mess upon the floor.

Aim your rifle at the target.

Fire your hose into the bowl.

Aim your rifle at the target.

Fire your hose into the bowl."

There was an astonished silence punctuated by snorts and giggles as they all tried very hard not to laugh. Ava pressed her lips together, trapping the chuckle struggling to explode out of her throat.

"Did you make that up?" Twitch asked, and the floodgates opened. Everyone roared with laughter.

"No! Of course not!" Terry's face was purple. "My mum used to sing it to me and my brothers when we were little. Anytime I go to the loo now, I hear it in my head. I never expected someone to film me singing it whilst I peed into some brambles." He shot Pam an evil look.

"I wouldn't really have put it on YouTube," Pam reassured him, wiping tears of laughter from her eyes. "Anyway, I've deleted it now."

As their laughter died away, there was silence. Ava's thoughts returned to the meeting that was happening below them.

"Do you think Thea Morton will let Rae keep Caliban?" Tara asked. "I hope so."

"I don't think they should be separated," Ozuru said. "That would be cruel."

"How long do ravens live?" Jack asked.

"In the wild, around ten to fifteen years," Twitch said. "But in captivity, it's more like forty."

"Wow! Rae and Caliban could be together until she's an old lady!" Tippi exclaimed.

The eight of them talked about the night the Dead Zoo Gang had come to Aves Wood until they heard a noise in the bathroom. They fell silent as Rae stepped out of the window to join them.

"Well?" Ava asked, and they all leaned forward.

"She's nice," Rae said shyly. "She's staying in a pub called the Sozzled Stork for the week. Marilyn's going to bring her back tomorrow and we're going to go for a walk. I thought we might go to Aves Wood."

"What about Caliban?" Ava asked. "Did she meet him?"

"I introduced them." Rae nodded. "I tried to make him do a 'boop boop' to her, but he got shy and tried to pull my hair out with his beak."

"Do you think she'll let you keep him?" Pam asked, turning the camera on Rae. "If you go and live with her, I mean?"

"Pam!" Terry chided. "Rae might not want to go and live with her!" He looked at Rae. "Do you think you might want to live with her?"

"I don't know." Rae blushed. "We only spoke for a bit. She's got a daughter called Lilly." She looked at Tippi. "She's the same age as you."

"You could have a sister!" Tippi clapped, and Ava grinned at her. "Sisters are great."

"Do you think Caliban would be welcome in her home?" Twitch asked.

"Maybe. She said she saw the connection between us and that she'd like to take me to the Tower of London to see the famous ravens there." Rae shrugged. "She asked me to make a list of the things she'd need to buy to take proper care of him."

"That sounds good," Tara said, glancing at Ava, who nodded.

"You could teach Lilly about birdwatching," Pam said, surprising everyone.

"Hey, I thought you said birdwatching was boring," Terry said.

"I don't remember saying that," Pam replied.

"Oh, you definitely did." Ava laughed. "At least a hundred times."

"And yet, here you are filming ravens and pigeons." Terry grinned maddeningly at her. "Because you think people will want to watch videos of them?"

"Well … yes…"

"And why would anyone want to watch bird videos, Pam?" Terry pushed.

"Because … well … birds are quite interesting." Pam lifted her nose in the air as if this was something she'd known all along.

"Victory!" Terry shouted, jumping to his feet. "Pamela Hardacre is a nerdy birder! We turned her into a proper Twitcher!"

ACKNOWLEDGEMENTS

This book is dedicated to our family cat, Kasper, who died of a heart attack whilst I was writing it. It was sudden, and a shock to the family. He helped me write so many books by sitting on my lap and purring loudly, or occasionally walking on my keyboard and deleting bits. It's only right I acknowledge the part he's played in my stories.

Sam Harmsworth Sparling is my first reader, my researcher and makes immeasurable contributions to all my books, listening to my late-night rants, laughing at my jokes (or frowning when they're not funny) as well as being my husband. His belief that I can do it always spurs me on and gets me over the finishing line. His protection of my writing time is invaluable. I simply couldn't write if it weren't for him.

Nearly all that I write starts in the real world and then takes an imaginative journey. This story is no exception. When I'm writing a book, which I nearly always am, I find it very hard to read fiction. Instead, I listen to podcasts. One of my favourites is called *This American Life*. One day, when I was travelling, I heard Episode #645. It is called "The Feather Heist", and was one of the most astonishing true crime stories I had ever heard. It was about the relentless work of investigative reporter Kirk Wallace Johnson, who became obsessed with the theft of over two hundred bird skins from the Natural History Museum. I bought his book, *The Feather Thief*, immediately and read it from cover to cover, the seeds of an adventure for my birdwatching detectives germinating in my head.

My book is not about an obsessive young flute player, but some of the facts from the case I've incorporated into my story. The Swan Museum is fictional and not the Natural History Museum in Tring, but it does borrow from it. I had a very enjoyable visit to the museum in Tring when researching this story. The bird exhibit is like the avian cast of The Twitchers series. I have been lucky enough to be schooled about the importance of museum collections from the senior curator in charge of insects at the Natural History Museum, Max Barclay, who is a personal friend and someone whom I find endlessly fascinating. Behind every single exhibit is an adventure; a story about how it was collected and came to be there.

In November 2019, thanks to bookseller Sue Chambers of Waterstones in the O2 Centre on Finchley Road, I met Christopher Skaife, the Ravenmaster at the Tower of

London. After our meeting, he took home my book about beetles and I took home his book about his life with the ravens in the tower, *The Ravenmaster*. It was my favourite book that year. I cannot recommend it highly enough. The ravens he takes care of are such characters, and I knew that one day I would write about one. His book inspired my Caliban, Rae's raven. I've watched many videos of ravens on YouTube. My favourite is about a raven called Fable. If you want to see how amazing these birds are, I recommend you go find it.

I'd like to thank everyone at Walker Books for letting me create a seasonal quartet for my birdwatching detectives. I'm very proud of this series. I hope young readers will enjoy it for years to come and appreciate the wonder of the birds they share the world with. It's been an utter delight to write these books. I have learned so much in doing it. Special thanks go to my editors, Megan Middleton and Denise Johnstone-Burt, and to Kirsten Cozens, PR goddess, for making sure everyone knows about this series of books.

I bow down to Paddy Donnelly, the artist who has created the covers for this and all four books in the Twitchers quartet. They are, without a doubt, the most beautiful and perfect covers. I'm so grateful and proud that he agreed to illustrate them. Special thanks to designer Ben Norland for doing such a superb job with the design.

And finally, thanks to Kirsty McLachlan, my agent, my friend, and the wind beneath my wings.

Discover the Twitchers'
first mystery adventure!

Twitch has three pet chickens, four pigeons, swallows nesting in his bedroom and a passion for birdwatching. On the first day of the summer holidays, he arrives at his secret hide to find police everywhere. A convicted robber has broken out of prison and is hiding in Aves Wood. Can Twitch use his talents for birdwatching in the hunt for the dangerous prisoner and find the missing loot?

WINNER OF THE CRIMEFEST AWARD FOR
BEST CRIME NOVEL FOR CHILDREN 2021

WINNER OF THE SAINSBURY'S CHILDREN'S
BOOK AWARDS 2021

A thrilling crime
for the Twitchers to solve!

When Jack rescues a wounded cat, he quickly suspects foul play.
Could there be a wildlife criminal on the loose in Briddvale?
Jack rushes to investigate, determined to catch the culprit, only
to stumble into a deepening mystery and a sinister criminal plot.
Can Jack and the Twitchers stop the villains before it's too late?

"A skilfully crafted mystery adventure.
A clarion call for environmentalists everywhere."

ROB BIDDULPH, *LOVEREADING4KIDS*

There's a thief in Aves Wood!

When the peregrine falcon nest is raided, Twitch realizes a thief is at work. Horrified, he and the Twitchers set out to catch the dangerous criminal, only to be ensnared in a deadly trap. Can they save themselves and stop the villain before anyone gets hurt?

"An exciting and edge-of-the-seat adventure."

READINGZONE

M. G. LEONARD is an award-winning, bestselling writer of children's books, as well as a member of Authors4Oceans. Her books are sold in 40 countries, and there is currently a TV series in development based on her Beetle Boy series. Her first picture book, *The Tale of a Toothbrush*, is out now. She is also co-author of the critically acclaimed Adventures on Trains series, and the author of The Twitchers, a mystery adventure series starring a group of birdwatching detectives. Before becoming a writer, M. G. Leonard worked as a digital media producer for the National Theatre, The Royal Opera House and Shakespeare's Globe. She lives by the sea with her husband, two sons and pet beetles.